A
RAILWAY
OF
DECEITFULNESS

A RAILWAY
OF
DECEITFULNESS

Written by R. L. (Rick) Hutchins

Contents

Acknowledgement

I thank the God of heanven and earth for giving me another opportunity to use my talent he has giving me.

And to the Lord christ Jesus who is the head of my life. And to my mother who struggle with me day and night as a child thanx to mom with love. And to my auntie B. Hutchins love you too. And to my siblings great love for you all. My church family may God continue to bless you all. And the Bell'sHutchins's family.

To the people at CSX Norfork Southern Union Pacific Santa fe Illinois terminal Burlington and Frisco thank you all for being a inspiration to me from the transit world movement. Trains are a hobbie of mines every since I was six year old. I would sit and watch a train and wandering in my mind where is it going.

And that's the amazing thing is you don't know But it's moving fast and with power. Trains are a unique way to travel and to transport loads from one state to the other. But some people think trains are fun to watch.

And to some they are considerabley dangerous if not watching carefully at rail crossing. But matter what trains will always be a hobbie of mines. And a certain blessing to the transit movement.

Runaway SD80

Chpt I

June 6 1980 in a small town of LaJunta Colorado where the population of 4 500 is the count with one sheriff and one deputy was all it took. A town where everybody knows somebody and everything you have done. And the people are still shook up about loosing a dozens of the towns friendlest people to a dangerous railroad crossing. The town has seen it's share of deadly train killings. But it's not over from being far fetch by the authority.

As it's first victims were the towns popular identical twins of LaJunta high Barry and Larry Chambers Barry was the high school's quaurterback who has made all american and a student with a 4.0 g.p.a. And Larry was LaJunta's all wide reciever with a 3.95 g.p.a. Both Barry and Larry was ahead of their class. But every average teen has mistakes in their life time some party to much some drinks more then others and there is the pot heads of the group. And one tittle of a mistake may cost them their life for not being careful.

And how train fatality are on a accelerating point: And Barry and twin brother Larry was only seventeen years of their prime. And death took their lives unexpected and forever missed. Now Barry was the oldest twin by five minuts then his brother. Larry was a little taller then Barry. They was a couple of great kids. But they both share a bad habits apiece.

Barry love to drink his cold beer with Larry loves his pot and both boy's enjoy girl's and joy rides. But the day of their demise was in a very peculiar way that seen no one can understand not even the law enforcement and investigator's that work the case. The car and the boy's bodies wasn't found near the railroad crossing the car was taken down the tracks with the boy's inside. The law enforcement agencies has gotten a report of a runaway locomotive that was moving at a speed of 65mph and nothing shouldn't be in it way.

Only one thing about this particular locomotive is a invisable spirit control it and no one can see it no one can stop it or get control of it neither it's plans is to kill and destroyed.

By 12 noon everyday this locomotive appear across from a corn field in front of Barry and Larry home to both boy's walk throughout the corn field until they both reach the locomotive and started throwing gravel at it. But no one was on it or around it it just was sitting idle. Then Larry climb on it while Barry yells at his brother. "Larry! Will you cmon here!" said Barry. "Coming Barry!" said Larry. As Larry did step off the steps of the locomotive it started coasting slow and quiet. And the boy's stood and watched. Without horns and no signals. The number's on the locomotive was 4311 but the number's was upside down spell hell was a sign of no conductor but a sign of a heated warning of wrath evil and a call of danger.

Now the locomotive pulls away down the track some hundred feet away from the crossing without horns and no signals flashing. To wait for it's next victim. With a loud crash and down the tracks it go with the victims. It won't move unless it dects a on coming car approaching to catch it's prey on it's tracks. Most of the corn field cloaks the body of the locomotive which make it extremely impossible to see it coming into veiw. Therefore the locomotive controls the signals and crossing gates but the signals and gates seem to be malfunctioning in which the locomotive keeps going down the tracks with it's victims in their vehicles trap. With the vehicles pushed thousands of feet down the track.

Before going into combustion of flames then the locomotive itself comes to a complete stop then it sounds it's horn for rejoice in killing another innocent victim's that cross it path.

As backing up from it's victim's with flashing light in front of it and upside down numbers flashing also h.e.l.l to let people know not to fool around with it. Now the time for the locomotive to go for another victim's. It listen to it's signal's from a radio scanner to let it know what's going on. Then it moves to detroyed the culprit that is trying to apprehend it. Or trying in other words to shut it down. This self possessed locomotive has power to control other locomtive's nearby for assisant into aid or support in killing those that impose it. Now Barry and Larry's deaths was a wakeup call for that there is something wrong seriously. And no one seems to know and to understand that this particular crossings had more fatal's then any other railroad crossing in the state. From the previous months and with the years as well.

Now Barry the twin that drinks and Larry is the weed smoker. But on June 6th of 1980 was a day of celebration for getting scholarship's from college's that recruited both twin's for academic's and degree's in physic's and engineering.

Barry was the one that shows;curiosity for matter energy and motion. With a degree in science would expand his learning for force. Now Larry was the one twin that has a mind to build and very skillfull in drawing some would call him a architect from the drafting classes he did sign up for in junior high. But both boy's were extremely skillful and full of talent and a lot of the world to discover. But their lives were cut short because of careless. And their bad habit's was with them both. Larry was extremely high on pot with Barry drinking like a horse and not aware of their surroundings and when larry came to that particular railroad crossings: he didn't brake at all. Barry told his brother to slow down when it came to that railroad crossings but he kept on going.

Therefore no signals no horns the locomotive plowed the boy's car thousand's of feet down the track with Barry and Larry inside with flames shooting from the vehicle being pushed on the rail's. And when the locomotive is done with it's kill it's horn will sound off as a glory way of evil deed is accomplished. And horns sounding loud means beware of danger and as the locomotive backs up to get the car off the tracks it would push the mangle vehicle off to the side of the track bed in a deserted field near Sha'vore county. Until some one will noticed the salvage of cars alone the tracks and on the side of Bentford's corn field.

Now Samuel and June Bentford has a farm near Sha'vore county;with 52.3 acres that run's alone the tracks: And on the opposite side of those tracks are cars smashed mangle and dead carcass that has being missing for awhile.

Therefore no one hasn't discover this catastrophe as of yet.

But the larger the rubble someone is bound to notices and the smell of dead carcass will not go unnotices. On July 22 of that day and that afternoon Mrs. Bentford did notice a unusual smell coming from the corn field. But couldn't recognize which end of the corn field where the corn stocks were tall to keep from seeing things on the otherside of the tracks.

This alarms the Bentford's quite clearly that someone is starting to put a salvage yard on the otherside of the tracks.

But wasn't notify at all of this transition.

It was eighty five degrees out and very humid to where Mrs. Bentford hung some laundry out to dry. And that's when she has notices that horrible smell coming from the direction of the tracks but she wasn't a nosey person that would snoop around to check things out: she left that up to Mr. Bentford as she marches into the house to informed him of the situation that is outside: "I will take a walk over to the tracks to see what going on". said Mr. Bentford. "Sam! You be careful over there". said Mrs. Bentford. As he begins to head out the back door the phone rings it was a call he must take to stay in business for himself. Mrs. Bentford looks at the clock it was 12:30 pm when she notice that locomotive was right on time that it was heard as she seen it from a distance from across the corn field. Just sitting there without anyone on it near the pile of rubble. But Mrs. Bentford knew something was spooky about this locomotive just sitting idle on hours. Now Mr. Bentford is off the phone but he have to go and take a look at a buddy's car to see what wrong with it.

So now the situation is on hold until Mr. Bentford returned which will be the later part of the evening. So just this one time that Mrs. Bentford decide to be nosey about the locomotive sitting and the horrible smell that is lingering so bad. Mrs. Bentford started to call the sheriff before taking a look herself but she started to show a bunch of curiosity by not letting the authority in on it. So she gear up with guts a brave woman she is. To go and investigate the situation herself which she had a whole lot of strength to walk with courage to investigate something that is not so familiar to see. As walking throughout the corn field with a lot of thoughts running through her mind telling herself to be careful at what you see: As she gotten close to the tracks the smell has gotten stronger with every step she has taken her curiousity was about to leave her but she must go on to discover what was going on. Now she was at the edge of the cornfield as she push all the tall stocks of corn out of her way to see and she was very stunned at what she had discover. A larger locomotive sitting near the salvage cars that was hit on the tracks and was pushed to the side of the tracks with seems to be dead corpse inside dead for awhile. "Hello!

Hello!" said Mrs. Bentford. All she got was her own echo not a person in sight and she walk around the locomotive twice but no one was there but as she was walking across the (track bed the locomotive started to move backwards towards her and Mrs. Bentford had enough strength to move from the tracks in time. Before it try to run her over."

You!

Son of b___h!" said Mrs. Bentford.

As the horns sound back while the locomotive coast backwards but only so many feet for Mrs. Bentford to cross in front of it so it can kill her then and there by running over her.But Mrs. Bentford was yelling at it before walking away.

As she walks back through the corn field angry with that locomotive trying to run her over but she didn't see no one on aboard that was the most mysterious thing to see a huge train run on it's own. Made things and the situation more interesting. As Mrs. Bentford walking back to her home cussing in a mean streak wandering why that train is doing here in a idle stage for a hour or two. And no one on board is a problem for things to happen. Not knowing there is a invisible evil being that is trying to take her life and those that are around her. As shaken up afterward's Mrs. Bentford didn't know who to tell about this mishap at the track moment's ago. To Mrs. Bentford she isn't laying down to this Mrs. Bentford thought of calling one of the ladies from her auxiliary to come and sit with her until Mr. Bentford returned.

Because she felt a little uncomfortable being by herself.

After that took place. Now she doesn't want to be alone and who is going to believe her if reported. But to Mrs. Bentford had to report what she saw near the tracks and the locomotive that looks suspicious without anyone on board. Well things just don't seems to be right at times but knowing to tell someone would be the right thing to do. Later on that evening Mrs. Bentford had to travel to the towns market for the local church pantry to replenished for the next day opening. As getting ready to go in the direction of the tracks that locomotive was waiting on her to cross at the right time. As Mrs. Bentford's car was approaching the tracks the locomotive did the unsuspected thing it plows into Mrs. Bentford's car dragging her down the tracks with her in it. With the impact killing her instantaneously on contact as she becomes a victim to the towns fatality of train killings.

Later that evening Mr. Bentford come home from a long day of hard work to a hot dinner. And not aware of his wife whereabouts so he thinks nothing of it he showers and put on something good to eat until Mrs. Bentford returned. As sitting down to eat in the kitchen the phone rings. With a member of the church pantry calling to see if Mrs. Bentford had gotten all of the food for the pantry. "hello the Bentford's residences". said Mr. Bentford. "Hi Mr. Bentford". "Is Mrs. June around if so can I speak to her?" ask the member. "Ah she isn't here for the moment". "But I'll have her to call you when she returned". said Mr. Bentford. Mr. Bentford notice the time has gotten later and his wife hasn't returned. So he started to wandering before calling on the local authority and getting them involve. Because his wife dosen't go out at night without him. He knows something isn't right. As he started to call around to see if anyone knows or seen his wife for her to call home. But no one hasn't seen her at all. So he calls his son and daughter to see if they have talk to their mother not knowing that his wife was murder it's very strange to leave home and not make it back and the family knows nothing about your whereabouts but knows their everyday routine's in their daily lives.

Therefore a whole week has gone by and no Mrs. Bentford and as Mr. Bentford still has not giving up;on the searchof his wife whereabouts and clues: that can leads to her disappearance. Now the couples children has gotten involved on the search for their dear mother and the local sheriff office has a countywide search with the next two counties. With no signs of abduction and no signs of her vehicle as the county detective's come in on the case with a solid motives on the disappearance of Mrs. Bentford but not really sure how the case may swing.

Now the sheriff that is elected in office not long ago is no other then Mr.Eugene T. Protzman T means Todd. The town elect Protzman for his integrity and honest leadership with the engineers club and has came on aboard to keep the town clean and rent of bad law violators by throwing them in jail.

This case seems to be very peculiar to the sheriff where he decides to take it upon himself to investigate sheriff has known the Bentford's for three decades. And now this don't seem to be right at all. But to find justice and recommend the laws are thrown the fullest. But still no human era in this particular case but a possessed machine will be a little hard to deal with in alone trying to stop it. This SD-80 runs on 3 000 gal fuel tank in which that is a lot of fuel to go the distance.

The First Stop

Chpt II

Next few days the locomotive went to the nearset city to part take in being a passenger train but to do worst damage in picking up passengers. But to kill as many passengers by bring them to a dangerous deserted area. As pulling the passenger car to a no where as all the passenger's are very confused and afraid because the train isn't stopping the passenger's was taking their last ride to their graves without no goodbye's as the locomotive use it's radio transmitter to call on other locomotive's for assistants in killing the passenger's on aboard. As men and women alike getting ready to die with children's included. As the locomotive sounds it's horn going down the track there were two other locomotive's running behind the passenger's car at 65mph with the head locomotive unleashed itself from the passenger's car taking a different track while the two locomotive's plows into the passenger's car killing everyone on board instantaneuosly by plowing the car into a train bumper post. The other two locomotive's combined weight and speed is a factor in this situation the passenger's notice the car just stop before being plow into by the other two locomotive's from the back and the impact killing all sixty two passenger's. But when the authorities and all law enforcements has shown up on a disastruos scene in which was a devastation to the people of the surrounding areas. Trying to piece to see what had happen as the railroad company was notify of these catastrophe as trains just don't have accident's daily but in this case there are trains that are jumping tracks and collision here and there. It was a nightmare for the entire state of colorado but it was the beginning and far from being over.

Now the runaway locomotive is making it way back to the it first disastruos area for more deadly task. As it listening to it's radio transmitter it knows that the railroad company is looking for it but it moves to stay at large to do more harm and deadly killings for it's joyous glory. Now sheriff Protzman had made the trip to where the train wrecks in the city of Hunterburg to help in on the investigation.

But parts of the puzzle is missing while the C.S.I and the F.B.I are trying to piece together at what had happen.It seem no one hasn't any answer's of yet. Now the railroad company representative's has shown up on the scene trying to see at what had cause the two locomotive's to plow into the passenger car like it did without any conductor's and engineer's on board is a darn good concern. As the investigator's walk throughout all the carnage looking at dead bodies being removed from the wreckage. Was a sadden thing to see and watch. It was very miserable for families to hear of a loss of a love one. Meanwhile the locomotive arrive back in Lajunta near that carnage:waiting on to make more of a dis aster. Back in Hunterburg at the scene of the wreckage the two representative's from the railroad company has dicussed about a certain locomotive is missing from the rail yard for weeks and almost a year but wasn't found at all. And now this situation has come knocking at their doors. "Wait a freakin minute!" said Sheriff Protzman. "You telling me you guy's have a runaway train at large!?" ask the Sheriff.

"Yes Sheriff." said one of the representative's. "It seems to me we hasn't recover it." said the other representative.

"Well! This train is causing a lot of havac and no one seems to know where to find it!" said the sheriff. "That is really hard to believe!" said the Sheriff. "We don't know how it just decide to leave the yard on it own. And no one seems to know it had disappeared as it coast from the rail yard." said the representative. "We just want the train back." said thee other repre. "Well we all have a job to catch this train." said Sheriff Protzman. Not knowing that this locomotive has came back to Sheriff Protzman district sitting idle near the crossing where it is destroying lives that crosses it's path of destruction.

As a on coming vehicle approaching the tracks the car came to a complete stop to see if the locomotive move. But no signals no horns for to yield at the crossing gates. So the indivual steps out of his vehicle to see if the locomotive is in the process of leaving. But no one was on the train the locomotive rev up it's engine's to move. But no one was on board. See the locomotive sat fifty feet plus from the gates to plow into it's victims on point to get to it's prey quick and in a hurry. Just like a cat and mouse game but a deadly situation at hand. But must be contained with all causes. How do you stop a machine from killing? How do you kill something that not a living soul? How can you bargain with it?.

Meanwhile back at the Bentford's the surrounding communities are pulling together;in the search for Mrs. Bentford. But don't know where to start. And Mr. Bentford looks out his back door and see that locomotive sitting. But never gave it a thought of checking it out and the back fields around the corn stocks: the smell stills lingering with a dead odour around the track area. As some of the rural area residences has noticed the lingering smell but doesn't recognize from which way it's coming from. Now it's going on a whole two months and no Mrs. Bentford;to where Mr. Bentford is giving up to where hope is all lost. Mr. Bentford is thinking in his mind that his wife has left him for another man in which she has comtemplating in earlier years But chosen to stay at home with Sam and put up with his ways.

As he stood up looking out his back door: acrossed the corn field that locomotive has disappeared one minute it seem to be there and the next it had coast off. Again Mr. Bentford hasn't gave any thought into his wife's intuition on the rubble and awful smell that just over the way.

A knock at the front door distract his way of thinking but as he go to see who it is surprisely it's his old and long time friend in the world Edward Dart of Dart's car parts inc has come to get some knowledge on what he is hearing about Mrs. June's disappearance. As Sam open the door to let Ed come into the house both men greeted each other with a hug of gladness as friends would do. "So Sam! How are you doing?" ask Ed. "Well my friend i'am sick to my stomach because my wife is gone." said Sam in a emotional state.

"And no one seem to know her whereabouts." said Sam.

"Sam! That's why i'am here to lend a hand in finding June." said Ed. "I'am really glad to hear that indeed you are a true friend and glad to see you again." said Sam. "Well Sam how long have we being friends?" ask Ed. "Well grade school." of course. said Sam. "So we being friends over forty plus years I say." said Ed. While talking another knock at the door it's the Sheriff stopping to check on Mr. Bentford to see if Mrs. Bentford has returned or any other news. As the important part of this situation is that everyone's is showing their concern's and pulling together for the care of a community figure. The Bentford's has being a voice in the rural area for more then fifty years. After thirty year in the army;he married June (Tills) Bentford in Southbend Indiana of May 7 1962. To Sam that was a great year for him and June newlywed in the prime of their lives then settle down with a son and daughter. Jon Leo Bentford is Sam's elder child with

Sheila Jennifer Bentford Silas as she is married to Jay Thomas Silas who is the town's CPA. Sam raised great children's to leave a legacy behind. By that his family means the world to him and his wife was his heart.

Sam literally worship the grounds she walked on. Now the evening is far fetch with all three men are reconnecting in the good old day's as being younger then they are now.

But there is a slight piece of the puzzle that is missing that is Mrs. Bentford and not just her but other's too. As the sheriff winds down with more information on the whereabouts of Mrs. Bentford and the others that are missing. As all three men call it a night the stranges thing happen the locomotive has returned and sitting quietly with it's lights off and Sam saw it but didn't say anything or mention it's suspicious of just sitting idle in that same spot without any boxcars without a caboose. And most of all no one is on board.

Later on that evening that locomotive has gotten another victim at it crossings and with that the death toll is even higher then the months before and no one has figure it out why is people being killed or missing or both? Now someone has suggusted that particular crossings should be shut off from crossing anytime soon: But Cornway Rd is the main road that leads to town and to the main street in the Lajunta area. To Sheriff Protzman the county would need to do a study on all the crossings for the safety of the people in the surrounding area.

Horns in the Night

Chpt III

As the evening turns late Mr. Bentford's home was quiet without Mrs. Bentford presence. While winding down to rest from his stressful day thinking that his wife would come through the front door in a second now but hasn't giving up on finding his wife. Because if June was there things was always right and Sam doesn't have to worried cause Sam knew that his wife had his back matter what June stood by Sam. As Sam was getting ready for bed he looks out to see if any animals messing around on his property or trying to disturb the chicken's. But what caught his attention was that locomotive just sitting in that same spot with no lights on in the dark fields:behind Mr. Bentford's home. Then Mr. Bentford went to his back door went out on the porch to see if he can see if anyone was on board.

But Mr. Bentford was going with his conscience by stay on his back porch because he might not like what he may see if he go and check it out. With how dark the corn field is it would've been impossible to see what was going on over at the tracks. Then suddenly the horns sounded as loud as it can if you were next to it. Like a tornado was about to hit the house that's how loud it was. As he just stood there trying to see if anyone was on board but with the corn stocks and the darkness of the back field Mr. Bentford's eye's just wouldn't let him see from where he was standing.

So Sam figured if he could walk a little closer;to his property line near the corn stocks he could get a better look at who's on board. Then the horns sounded even louder as sam gotten a little close to the corn field. Therefore the locomotive felt a presence near the corn field. Now it's engines turn on to move away from it's resting place. Finally mr. bentford could see the windows to see if anyone was on board. Sam looked hard to see who's was on board and he saw no one but a spirit with red eye's looking out at him standing there.

Sam eye's gotten big from what he just saw up in the window's of the locomotive as Sam headed back in a hurry and as his heart pumping faster his leg's started to give out on him before he could reach his back porch when he came up on his porch sam was exhausted from the field to his porch.

Sam went inside to call Ed insteaded the sheriff office.

Sam calls Ed to tell him what he exactly saw it was very very disturbing to him. Sam calls Ed because he can confined in Ed not to say a word. See if Sam would've walk more steps then he did he would've discover he wife's car and her body inside decaying. But he didn't go any further causes what he saw in the windows of the locomotive. When Sam got inside the door he grab the phone while dialing Ed's number Sam was looking out over the corn field he notice the locomotive was starting to coast slowly backward towards the crossing's all by itself sounding it's horn and flashing it's lights. As Sam was hanging up the phone in which he didn't finished dialing Ed's number from watching the locomotive backup slowly. Now in Sam's mind. Who is going to believe him? Or what to say about this freaky situation. As sitting down at the kitchen table Sam couldn't stop thinking about what he just saw to he couldn't sleep at all.

With enough on his mind. Sam seem to be going through a mental stake from thinking about his wife's whereabouts and now this creature aboard a killer train. The next day that engine was back in this same spot but Sam has to have the courage: like his wife did when she was alive to go to check it out. But Sam just don't have the gut's to do it. So Sam decides to walk out to his barn to check to see if anything looks suspicious in there but of course a family of possums and a couple of barn owl's. But nothing out of the ordinary.

As he was going into the barn he reconized that same stinch that was coming from one side of the corn field. And one more thing that Sam has notice was the pile of rubble was getting absolutly bigger then before: But Sam wasn't trying to be a nosey person by investigate a lousy smell and a pile of rubble. Standing in the doorway of his barn looking to see if he can do something to inquire the smell that is lingering so badly. All a suddenly Sam heard a train engine coming from the west but a different locomotive with boxcar's going throughout the rural area. But there was a conductor on board as he wave at Sam from a distance and sounding his horn and the signal's were working and no accident's.

Sam returned a friendly wave with a kind smile and a slight thought of his lovable June how they both would wave at the trains when going by. And he remember june would ask him "where do you think it's going?" ask June. And Sam would reply. "I don't know but it's going." said Sam. As they both just stood there looking as the train passing by and wandering in their minds where is this train going. That's Sam remininscing of the good old days but nothing spoils the moments to think of his precious June the mother of his children. Now June has being missing a month and no recovery of her no where it's like she has left the face of the planet.

But in a weird way and Sam is still getting calls from people all over asking "have she returned " or "any word on Mrs.June?"Asking concern people of the communities.

As of one day out of the week Jon and his sister Sheila come to check up on their father's well being since their mom is gone. To where Jon started to show signs of aggressive and frustration's out on anyone who looks like they would know the whereabouts of his mother's well being. As Sam talking with his son to let him know that him and his sister Sheila is all that he has now as Sam starts to get emotional just thinking about his precious June. "Damit! It's hurts so bad without her here in our lives!" said Sam. As Jon stood up next to the coffee table thinking to himself that mom's killer is still out there. While Sam in tears Jon is convinced that it would take the two of them to help catch June's murderer. "But we don't know if she is dead or not." said Jon.

As Sam looks up at his son "What are you thinking son?" ask Sam. "I'm thinking that mom might be alive." said Jon.

"But don't know where to start".said Jon. Now the phone is ringing and Jon go's to answer it with his sister Sheila on the other end asking her brother if him and her dad was ok and have the both of them eaten yet. Because Sheila is a great cook in her own way with the help of her mother June teaching and showing her how and what to do when she is on her own and married. Sheila has fix a savory meatloaf with a thick gravy and pinto beans with potatoe salad. Jon asking. "what time is dinner?" "when you and dad decide to get here" said Sheila. (chuckling) "By the way any news on mom's whereabouts?" asking Sheila.

"No not yet." said Jon. "But we will be there soon." said Jon. Before hanging up the phone. Then all of suddenly sam looks at his son with a strange look and ask his son to follow him to the kitchen to show him this special locomotive that just sit idle on hours in the same spot on the otherside of the corn field. "If I tell you something please don't repeated." said Sam. "Tell me dad!" said Jon. With excitement.

"Look!" said Sam. "You see that engine just sitting there?" asking Sam. "I went out one night to see who was on it and little that I knew was something on it that wasn't a human being." said Sam. "But those eye's were frightening enough." said Sam. "Dad! What in the hell are you talking about!?" asking Jon. "What you are saying doesn't make any sense at all!" said Jon. "Like I said Jon don't repeat it." said Sam. "Dad! Maybe I should check it out also." said Jon.

"I hope that you would see for yourself." said Sam. Therefore Jon knew then that his father's words was also true enough to check it out to see if his father was right about everything. As Sam sat down at the kitchen table gazing at the kitchen floor and mumbling words to himself as jon can see that his father is going through a lot. First June. And now this creature on this train. Sam thinks it's all a big dream of course a nightmare.

As both father and son leave to join Sheila and her family for dinner and discussed June's funeral service if they can recover her remains if found. With June's disappearance is a disappointment to the family as much as to the community.

Just like the popular twins and one's before that. But on the way to Sheila's home Sam was telling his son Jon about that particular locomotive and the horns in the late night hours causing him many nights of sleep. And the engines are loud to where it vibrates the windows only if the family knew that this particular engine has taken the wife and mother of this family. Then justice will be served in a unusual way: Because it's a machine that can't be bargaining with. Until someone can climb aboard and apprehend the blackbox to relief the spirit that is in full control of the throttle but one thing this spirit is very evil and wicked and kill at will only if it sense anyone near the locomotive. So how can a killer train be stop? "Son! It's something about that train sitting there everyday just idle without anyone on board." said Sam. "I have a funny feelings that the train had something to do with your mother's death." said Sam. "Well dad we need to check this situation out and get Euggene involve since he is sheriff." said Jon. "Wait a freakin minute son!" said Sam. "what did I say earlier to you!?" ask Sam. "Not one word to nobody!" said Jon. "Ok! nobody son!" said Sam. "Your mother gave me strength and we both was strong together in this community." said Sam."

Now I don't need the people of this community to look at me like i'm a crazy idiot." said Sam. "So you and I are the ones to check things out ourselves?" asking Jon. "Because in so many words that this locomotive had something to do with mom's disappearance or death then what are we going to do dad?" ask Jon.

"I think we should checkout that locomotive before telling the authorities." said Sam."I was going to tell Ed about it but Ed gossip like a woman."said Sam. "Oh not a word to your sister." said Sam. "Ok dad." said Jon. In deed Jon's mind is to doing the right thing by getting the law official involved in this matter. But Sam has a conscience that runsaway at times but means well. Therefore the men are getting even closer to finding out what really happened to the wife& mother of both men. And just a day ago that locomotive has claimed another victim at that same crossing's to sheriff himself has order no one shall cross there. Until further notice. To have the signals check to see if any malfunctional is creating a havoc in crossing's the tracks.Or the signals work when there is no train not working when there is a train. Either way someone is being killed at this track crossing's.

Track Bed of Blood
Chpt IV

Now Lajunta is in a peace vigil for the town's lost of the people over the years. And the sheriff and the deputy are keeping things in order throughout the ceremony. And Sam and both of his children did attend for their mother and wife.

And which was very pack and crowded but everyone was joining hands and humming in tune as tears were shed. As the crowd started to disband to go home people were reaching for others to greet one another with a friendly hug and something kind to say to someone else who have lost a love one in a tragical way. It was hard to listen to others stories about how they lost a dear and close friend or a love one. As the crowd went their separted ways so did Sam Jon and Sheila and her family Sam and Jon had road together going back home to go to see what's on the other side of the tracks to do their own investigating. And to see where does it lead them.

As returning from the vigil rally coming down the narrow country road before turning onto the dirt driveway sam and Jon had stop in the middle of the road to check out the barriers that was place at the crossing's near the house. Seeing that there was a couple of representative's looking and checking for malfunctioning of the signals and gates. But everything was working in a perpective way then looking down the tracks no signs of problems but both men notice that the tracks going down towards the corn field were damage from skits marks like something was push with force. Or plowed so many feet down the tracks. And the white gravel is full of human DNA which was very confusing to both of the representative's. And Sam and Jon both went to talk to both representative's about a locomotive that just sitting on hours idle in this particular spot down the track behind his home on thee other side of the corn field. The both of the representative's had explained to Sam and Jon that sometimes the locomotive would rest or stop here until it get a signal to move from the central office in florida. By looking down the tracks no sign of any train insight. As all four men standing there looking in the direction where the locomotive usaully parks but very skeptical about all the rubble that was on the far side of the second set of tracks.

Therefore all of the evidences was clear out all in one day which was impossible to see. "like how could this be?" ask Sam. "what do you mean sir?" ask one of the representative.

"Because we been up and down this tracks and no signs of problems or troubles. "Hey we saw where there were mangle up cars down on the other side of the second set of tracks sir." said Sam. "You can see the rubble from the back door of my house." said Sam. "Well guy's we haven't seen anything coming from that direction." said one of the representatives. "S—t!" said Sam. "Well sir we are looking for a runaway train in which we haven't found but we are still looking for it." said thee other representative. Sam and Jon just looked at both men and started walking back toward the car to getting in to head to the house.

But Sam and Jon knows deep down in their hearts that the locomotive had something to do with the silent deaths that happened to most of the town's citizens including june's disappearance or death. As walking in the front door both Sam and Jon heard a train engine coming from the other way: with boxcar's and a caboose behind. And immediately, Jon went running out of the back door to see what will happen's if the train stop but it kept going. "Oh what a relief to see it keep on moving!" said Jon. "Because if it stops!

I'am going to see what's it problem for stopping here so much!" said Jon. "Son! Be careful not to get into any danger." said Sam. "I lost my wife I can't afford to lose you and your sister." said Sam. "Wait a minute it's slowing down for whatever reason." said Jon. As Jon take off the back porch and not thinking: that this creature could harm him in so many ways and not know it.

"Jon!' "Jonny!!" calls Sam. Suddenly Jon stops and turns to look at his old man in the face then turns and looks at the train as it starts to move again: down the track until it was completely out of sight. As Jon started to walk towards the house he notices the awful smell that was coming from the direction of the corn field but he saw nothing that coexist with that lingering scent. So Jon decides to walk towards the tracks and he discover the more he walks near the tracks stronger the smell when Jon got right up on the track bed there it was a track bed full of blood and parts of the human anatomy. But as long as Jon stood there the more he become sick of the smell until he started to regurgitate with gaging until his eye's tearing up keeping him from seeing well. As Jon trying to make his way back to his father house his sight came back all Jon can think of was his mother. When Jon reaches the back porch of his father's house. Jon falls to his knees as he crying out loud until Sam comes out on the porch to see why his son is crying. "Jon! Jonny! What a matter? What did you see!?" asking Sam. "Jon! Cmon what did you see!?" asking again Sam. "Blood and body parts." said Jon. As Sam stood over his son looking down on him to where Sam was also speechless. Because Sam seen this creature face to face from a distance.

Now both father and son had snapshots of what's going on in their own backyard to they can piece everything on their own or take it to the sheriff. Some how the pile of rubble is gone. What or who? Has left blood and body parts near the tracks. Sam helps Jon up off the porch into the house.

"Dad! We aren't safe here." said Jon. "Well son What are you supposing we should do?" ask Sam. "What I saw was despicable and disgusting." said Jon. "So what i'am saying dad is you don't need to be here alone by yourself." said Jon. "Look son! Your mother and I had this house built to raise you and your sister to have a better life and damn it! if i'am going to let some damn creature on a train run me off because it ain't happening." said Sam. "i didn't see no creature dad I saw blood and body parts!" said Jon. "Dam it son!

What difference does it make what you saw." said Sam.

"We have to convince others that something is wrong here." said Sam. "Dad! You are right who is going to believe us?" ask Jon. As both men are traumatize so often by the things they both was expose to that has a bitter and nasty memory inside of their heads will always be with them.

As the night begins Jon just sit's on his father's sofa just gazing at the back door like someone was coming in for a talk with him and Sam was in the kitchen trying not to think about his situation anymore. Because it makes matters more vulnerable and difficult to defend. So therefore both men is holding evidents to many cases and not realize they are the key witness to a crime that is in their own backyard. As one convinced the other not to say a peek. But before the crack of dawn Sam needed to go to the bathroom to wash his face from sweating so much from nightmares of losing his entired family and also friends. Which was no one left but him and the spirit on the train. As he was taking a moment to look in the mirror he saw more grey hairs then he saw in previous months but it didn't bother Sam at all Sam knew that he is living a great and healthy life.

Now coming out of the bathroom Sam stops in the hallway to listen in on a train coming towards the house but couldn't reconized the direction it was headed: so Sam went to his back door to look and see which direction it was headed. But little he knew it was engine 4311 doing it's usual stop on the second set of tracks right behind the corn field. As Sam trying to wake his son Jon from his deep sleep to let him know that the locomotive is back. "Jon! Jonny! Get up! The locomotive is back son!" said Sam. As Jon sit's up on the sofa looking like he had a rough night while tossing and turning fighting in his sleep saying out loud "Getaway!

From me please don't hurt!" said Jon. "Morning dad." said Jon. "Son! Hurry for that locomotive decides to take off please." said Sam. "Ok dad How long has it been sitting out there?" ask Jon. "Let's say for awhile." said Sam. Now roughly it would be about two hundred yards to the tracks itself from Sam's backyard thru the corn field then the tracks.

As the locomotive sits on scheduled to wait for it's next prey at the crossing's. But it doesn't know that the crossing's are closed for safety and further notice from the sheriff's office. So while sitting there the spirit has sense a couple of individual's coming near the engine as both men walks around the engine just trying to figure out what's going on. As Jon walks on the otherside of the locomotive Sam took the otherside: as Sam stumble upon a license plate that looks familiar to him near one of the rails "Huh! This looks like June's plate on her car." said Sam. The minute he said that the locomotive starts to coast off very slowly back in the direction it came." Jon!! calls Sam. While Jon was standing on the otherside Jon decides to look up at the window of the locomotive and saw a demonic looking creature gazing back at him with red eye's and a canine smile was very spooky to Jon as it was to his father. As the locomotive moves on down the track Sam and Jon ran and hug each other.

"Dad I saw that creature you was talking about." said Jon.

"Now you believe me?" ask Sam. "Dad I didn't even doubt you in the first." said Jon. "Maybe it would've be nice that I check it out for myself." right? Said Jon. "Well absolutely." said Sam. As both men stood there looking in the direction of the engine is going they notice the engine has stop further up the track and passed the crossing's just sitting there.

"Hey dad you think we can catch it?" ask Jon. "Me running after a locomotive son! C'mon you no better then that." said Sam. (both men laughing). "Did you see that the locomotive coast through the crossing's without it's horn and the signals and gates didn't function like it suppose to?" ask Jon. "Damn!

You are right Jonny." said Sam.

"Well it will be back you can count on it." said Sam. "Now it knows we are on to it now." said Jon. As both men headed back to the house thinking and conspiring how they are going to catch this ridiculous looking creature with red eyes and a mouth full of teeth will be a adventurous.

Fog of Death

Chpt V

Now the fall weather is beautiful this time of year in Lajunta where the trees are a spectacular display throughout the county. And the mountains are also remarkable to look upon.

But there is one thing the citizens do respect is the heavy fog in early morning hours to the city has to shut down be cause of it's fog in which is dangerous and hazardous to try to drive in. It was 4:30 am on a saturday morning when a janitor by the name of Terry Erickson was leaving for work a little bit early so he can stop for a bite for breakfast at T&R beer House on the corner of Eugenio and Bess road. Little that Terry knew that the news is for a two hour delay for the city of Lajunta road to stay clear. As Terry wasn't on the road for five minutes: when the fog over took his visiability to keep on driving even while his brights were on the fog still was to much for him. As Terry was near the crossing's near Sam's house the fog gotten even thicker to he couldn't even see the crossing's. BANG!! A loud noise in the fog Terry ran into engine 4311 into the crossing's to where Terry's car blow up instantaneously with him inside.

And the locomotive starts to pull off going in the opposite direction leaving another victim dead.

The crashed has woke up Sam and Jon both wandering what was that noise they both heard. "Dad it sounds like a crash but I can't see anything with this thick fog." said Jon. "You smell that son? It smell like something is burning." said Sam.

"Well let's get dress and check it out." said Sam. When Jon looks out the side window of the house he saw a ball of fire but still couldn't make out what was burning. While Sam was on the phone to place a 911 call for help but the lines were busy from all the backed up calls that were coming throughout the county from accident's in the morning hours. Finally Sam got through to the dispatcher: to let them know of a accident that just happen on corn way road.

"Hello this is Mr. Sam Bentford i'am calling to let you know of a accident that just happen out on cornway road the car must be in flames we really can't see to well in this thick fog." said Sam. "We will send the e.m.s out sir." thank you.

Said the dispatcher. The locomotive sat there intentionally just in case for someone to run into it. That's how thick the fog is to where it's causing accident's everywhere in the county.

Now the fire truck's paramedic's and law enforcements are on the scene trying to see what in the world did the vehicle hit? Because there isn't no train. As Jon and his father has walk up on the scene to give their input on the accident. "Hey Deputy! we know what happen see this person did run into this particular locomotive which was sitting in the crossing's the fog was so thick this person couldn't see in front of himself so he slammed into the locomotive. Now Sheriff Protzman has shown up on the scene. As the fire department put out the flaming car and try to pull a burned corpse of Terry Erickson. Now the sheriff department are trying to figure out who is this individual in this burned vehicle "So call the cornor's office and tell them we need them a.s.a.p." said the sheriff. While the sheriff come over to interview the Bentford's to get some knowledge on what happen and the Bentford's told the sheriff about this particular locomotive that sit's in this vicinity quite often as much as possible. But don't know why this part of the tracks it's here.

"Do you guy's know what this engine looks like? I mean the color and numbers." said the sheriff. "Well absolutely sheriff the numbers was upside down and it was black on red with a saying on it (let's go to hell) on the side of it." said the Bentford's. "Let's go to hell was on it?" ask the sheriff.

"Yes sir sheriff." said Jon. And the sheriff has realized the locomotive they are discussing about is the same one that is missing from the rail yard over in Sha'vore county. "I believe that's the same locomotive that maybe involved in the twin boy's that lives across the street from you Sam." said the sheriff. "Sheriff tell us what is really going on? Ask Sam. "Mr. Bentford I don't really know but I will get to the bottom of this because it's a mind boggling situation that's must be restrained quick and in a hurry." said the sheriff.

"Sheriff! Jon and I was out there at the tracks walking around that locomotive and I stumble upon a license plate that I believe is June's it from her car." said Sam. "why was it out there?!" ask the sheriff. "my goodness this case is getting crazy by the minutes." said the sheriff. "Your guess is as good as mines." said Sam. "I'am thinking if that's the same locomotive that had something to do with that Hunterburg massacre also that happen a month ago." said the sheriff. As standing near the scene the cornor's office is now on the scene talking with the sheriff and detective's about the victim's identity to where they couldn't get a positive I.d on the victim and the vehicle. "My my what a lost." said the sheriff. As talking to the detective's. When pulling the victim out of the burn vehicle the corpse fail apart by taking it from the vehicle. As the neighbors were watching things the sheriff made everyone to go home because the scene was a little disturbing to others. As the sheriff talks to one of the C.S.I's about the identification of the victim and how soon can the sheriff office expect the paper work? "What in the world happen?" ask C.S.I. "I truly believe the heavy thick fog had something to do with it." said the sheriff. "Did anyone else knows what had happen?" ask C.S.I. "Wait a moment the Bentford's heard it when the victim had crashed." said the sheriff. "but they didn't see a thing because of the fog." said the sheriff.

"Hey sheriff! Did you get a report on that missing engine that left the rail yard over in Sha'vore county?" ask C.S.I.

"Yes I did and I think that this locomotive is what we are looking for." said the sheriff. "Because the Bentford's has seen it a numeral of times down behind the corn field sitting idle." said the sheriff. Now as the sheriff the deputy a investigatorfrom the county and C.S.I had all took a walk down the stretch of tracks to do some looking around to find something to build a case to catch a murdered that's on the loose. But little that they all knew this is not a average murdered but very unusual to put it. Now Sam and Jon are loo -ing on from the back porch of the house watching the sheriff and the other parts of the law at work and dig for evidents to help to build a case. Therefore all the men were doing their share of work and the sheriff had stumble upon a spot that is satuarated with blood in certain parts of the track bed and human body parts at the second set of tracks. "Well guys it looks like a crime scene to me." said the sherriff. "So I take it that someone or something has done something bad out here." said the sheriff. As both Sam and Jon has walk up to the crime scene from a distance to their home to ask questions about what's going on. "Sheriff! We need to know the truth and what the hell! Is going on?" ask Sam.

"Ok I need for the both of you to returned to your home and I will be there to talk with you both a little later." said the sheriff. So both father and son turned around to returned to the house thinking that they should know exactly what's going on. But truly the Bentford's know's more about the whole scenario then the authorities but rather keep quiet as usual among themselves.

Now as Sam looks at his watch to determine the time the engine will appear while the authorities are on the tracks to see if the locomotive appear right on time. As the sheriff and the other parts of the law were wrapping up for the evening but not quite yet. As the men all looking in the direction of the rail crossing's and gates and they all saw was a bright light miles down the track but it stop for some reason but the sheriff and the other parts of the law was waiting on it to arrived near the corn field as it would on other days. So Sam and Jon both walking fast to tell the sheriff that it's time for it to be here in it's usual spot. Now the locomotive has starting to back up and go to another area of the vicinity. Because it has detected a sense of the law down the tracks meddling. While the men were packing up to leave from a chaotic scene they all witness the engine didn't come forth so the law can look and check things out.

"So sheriff! What now!?" ask Sam. "Well we wait for it but if it want come here then we will go to it." said the sheriff. As all the men including the Bentford's started to walking towards the locomotive when they all heard the engine sounding loud and started moving towards all the men's.

And moving pretty fast for not to stop at all the locomotive kept going pass the men without a sound of a horn or no signal's. And Sam shouted "Sheriff!! that's the one!!" said Sam. "Hey guys! That's our culprit right there!" said the sheriff. "Did any of you see it in the window?" asking Jon.

"i saw something that look like a sort of a creature like." said one of the C.S.I. As all the men looking in the direction of the engine as it disappear out of sight.

Now all the men were on board and saw the same thing that the Bentford's had a brief run in with but they both was shook up and shock about it. And now that the cat is out of the bag on this case but far from being over for the Bentford's. Therefore the evening is upon them to wind down from a accident early that morning to a creature aboard a engine later on in the day.As Sam and Jon were going into the house they both stop in there steps to listening for another sound of a engine coming from the same direction so both men went back out the back door to see what will transpired. The engine got louder while pulling with a lot of power. But not the same engine. This engine had boxcars and a caboose. As the night get later some how the weather changed drastic with another heavy fog moving in to the area. Now the fog has returned so did engine 4311. It pull in it's usual spot in back of the Bentford's home. Actually this time the creature exit the engine for a little retribution for knowing to much was to get one of the men for a prey. So it exit the engine and walk towards the back of the Bentford's house to drag one or both men even better then just one.

Now that it reaches the back door just standing and gazing into the kitchen and then the kitchen windows wandering where is it prey.

As it walks around to the front of the house it decides to stand on the front porch and sniff at the door: like it can smell through the door. While sniffing it looks over through the front window at Jon while he is at sleep gazing and sniff the window as Jon lays on the sofa then it walks further around the house and then it spotted Sam in the bed. The creature is 7'6 and very cleaver and only thing it's know to do is to kill with every intention as evil would do. As the creature was walking back to the engine it step on a live trap a trap that Sam had put to catch coyote's and other vermin's that will prey for game the creature sqeeled and grawled it grawled so loud both Sam and Jon woken up. But the creature left with the trap on it paw as every step it took was blotches of blood from it's paw. Now it's really mad so it will returned for either Jon or his father. To the creature one must die for getting the law involved and for the trap that hurt it's paw. Next day there was blood in the backyard leading back to the railroad tracks. "Dad! Come and look!" said Jon. "what do you know that s.o.b was here on our property." said Sam. "I would call the sheriff but i'm not going to now." said Sam. "Dad what are we going to do?" ask Jon. "Son! We are going to do the job." said Sam. "This thing played with us far to long so we aren't going to play anymore with it!" said Sam. "Truly! Son I think that thing had something to do with your mother my wife is gone!!" said Sam. As Sam started to get emotional by thinking about his wife. While Jon come over to his dad and comfort him from his anger point. "So no more playing around son." said Sam.

Face to Face with the Enemy
Chpt VI

Now Sam and Jon are trying not to spill anything that the creature was on the property and got hurt by one of the live trap's near the house. As Jon went to look in the barn for a similar trap to replace the one that was taken by the creature. Instead of grabbing the trap and setting it Jon picks up his father's assult rifle that he keeps in the barn and one in the house for protection and just in case. As Jon calls his dad outside in the backyard to show him the old hardwear that he stored in the barn. "Oh yeah! That was the good and excellent days son." said Sam. Now Sam did kept all kinds gun's and rifle's but never had to use them at all. But both men has a funny feeling that they may need to use them real soon. Because the day is far fetch and their lives are on the line. To both father and son it is what it is. Do or die. Say the last name then explained to everyone that you isn't laying down to no one especially something that is at the bottom or middle of the food chain. "Dam if I let this so call creature from the train run us off."S—t! Said Sam. So both father as well as the son has gotten all the ammunition along with every gun from sam's gun safe. But if no one knew any better you would think that both men were getting ready for a world war: "But coming to face to face with with this thing giving me a sore head." said Jon."Son! Don't give up now." said Sam"Jonny who is that in the drive way?" ask Sam. "It's Sheila dad." said Jon.

"What in the world is she doing here?" ask Jon. Up the steps into the house she go's. "Hey dad! Jonny! I just stop by to see how my family is doing." said sheila. "what's with all the fire power?" ask Sheila. "We are going hunting." said Sam. "Just don't bring back a monster for me to cook it." says Sheila. As both men looks at each other in a strange way that they both understood what must be done. It's seem that Sheila knew what was going on. "Dad Jonny. Do you both need anything for me to do?" ask Sheila. As both men just looks at her while they both listening for that engine that is coming up the track now. Jon and Sam both go to the back door and looks out to see what happens next. "Guy's! what is going on here?" ask Sheila. As she follows them to the kitchen and now all are gazing out the back door to see if that train would stop: "why are you guy's watching a train?" ask Sheila. "Ok! Dad Jonny! Will you both be honest with me I like to know what's going on!!?" ask Sheila again. As both men just look at each other before speaking anything about the truth between june's disappearance until a night ago there was a mysterious creature on the property.

But Sam didn't know where to begin telling his precious daughter about anything that himself and Jon has been through. "Sheila dear you know that locomotive that just stops out here just on the other side of the corn field?" ask Sam.

"Yes! What of it?" ask Sheila. Sam starts to get emotional about June's disappearance. "We think that had something to do with your mother's disappearance." said Sam. "what!?" say's Sheila. As Sheila slowly sits down at the kitchen table looking like she can kill the next person or thing that comes through the door. "How so dad!?" ask Sheila. As she become emotional as well.

So now the family wants revenge for a wife and a mother.

"You telling me that a locomotive had something to do with mom's disappearing?" ask Sheila(while crying). "that's bullsh--!! dad!" said Sheila. "Well honey that's a possibilities that could've happen." said Sam. That the Bentford's are a well known family in the rural area of colorado. But June was the sweetest woman that you every wants to meet with a lot of love to go around to everyone she comes in touch with. "So! We need to nail! This f-cker!! for mom's sake!!" said Sheila. "We are going to get him whatever it is: I will split it's dome wide open!" said Sam. As jon sat quietly on the sofa thinking how to lower it into a trap where it can't get out. And not knowing that this creature can also camouflage itself invisible for a weapon to use on it enemy.

But Jon knows he need more facts on this creatures well being before trying to trap it. Or going after it. "Hey Jonny!

Did you sat that trap next to the house like I asketh?" ask Sam. "Yes dad I did." said Jon. "I hope that I be here when you both pop him so I can give it a kick in the groin area." said Sheila. As this family take heed in getting prepared to do battle with a unwanted visitor from hell. Is something that the family had no intentions of going up against. While everyone was sitting around waiting for an ideal among the three there was a knock at the door and the father as well as the son had reach for a weapon for anything that comes through that door was a target. As Sheila walks over to the door and looks to see who it was: it was Edward Dart come to see his best friend since grade school and to see if any thing on Mrs. Bentford's whereabouts.

As Ed enter he greeded everyone with a hug and smile. And then started picking with Sheila and Jon. By telling both Jon and Sheila howthey use to run and climb on everything that was insight to where Jon climb the tree in front of the houes until he couldn't see him anymore. "Hey. What's up with all the fire power?" ask Ed. As the Bentford's household turned silent with an instant. While each one was looking and trying not to speak: With Sam changing the subject. "Hey Ed what brings you over here?" ask Sam. "You my friend. I was thinking about you and the kids and I do missed June a whole lot." said Ed. "But I hope things are going well for you and the kids."said Ed. "If not i'm just a call away my friend." said Ed. As the night approaching quite fast the Bentford's are ready to go to war with a unwanted tall and hairy big paws red eye's and talon's having evil creature. That has target the Bentford's for some reason but they are ready to do battle with. And the real reason is that both father and son are both prey in the creature's eyes of evil to where it must have both men or one then the other.

With the fall season coming it gets dark pretty quick with the weather and the trees changing beautiful colors. As the tone is set at the Bentford's house. Waiting on this particular creature to show up for a blast he shown up in a unusual way: that the family wouldn't thought of or cross anyone's minds. As Sam tells his daughter Sheila to go home and him and Jon deal with this evil sucker. Sheila refuses to leave her family in danger. But she rather stay and help fight off some evil creature that has being targeting her family.

"Sheila! Please darling I need for you to let the sheriff know what had happen here if anything happens with your brother and I." "So go!!" said Sam. As Sheila runs out of the front door in tears to where she couldn't see straight.

But Sheila did the unthinkable by sitting in her vehicle and not make a peep or movement. As the creature parks the locomotive to where no one can see it from the one side of the corn field. Unless you are coming and going across the tracks to where ever. Now the creature has made it's way to get it prey for to survive off of as getting close to the house it camouflage itself from it's prey to make it's victims defenseless and blind. So the day that the locomotive was going places and killing people and harming others. But people say that the train was moving by itself or no conductor and no engineer's were on board. It's because it made it self invisible to it victims. With this way it makes it hard to fight what you can't see. But the creature do have a weakness also. Time is a weakness if not fed before the next nightfall it starts to stank bad with a hollow body that can move in any kinda way. Now it's close to being face to face with a enemy the Bentford's are enemy to this creature and this creature is the enemy to the Bentford's. It killed sereval of people over the pass years. With Mrs. June Bentford as a senseless and loving person which died for nothing. Was a victim of this creature.

As it makes it way up on the back porch it's looking into a dark house but sees no one insight so it's sense of smell is very and highly sensitive. And it smells both men but don't see them. While both men are hiding in the house Jon can see at the back door to where it's trying to come in on them. As the creature starting to push on the door to get in to feed on one or both men and be done with it. And go on to the next victims. Now it's getting agravated because it came here for one thing and one thing only to feed on these humans that got the authorities involved and invading in on it's terroritory at the tracks and seen it's face up in the locomotive windows. So it seen them it smelled both men from a distances. And now it wants them both. As Sam is at the front of the house waiting for the creature to come thru the front door to start blasting at it with all he has got. But Sam started moving around in the house. He looks out the livingroom window and turns mad as hell. Because Sheila's car is sitting in the driveway with her in it. By now the creature has made it's way around to the front of the place. And Sam lying back down on the floor with his weapon on the door and windows hope for it to come on into the house.

As Jon and Sam notice how quiet it became Sam had gotten up and looked out to see what had happen and the creature is between the front porch and Sheila's car. Just standing there looking at the house but not only did it smell the men it smells Sheila too. As it slowly walks over to her vehicle and then looks at her while breathing hard and taking in her scent. As Sheila sat still and not make a peek wandering how can it get inside to get her out of the car. The creature has paws and not hands. But it used it's talons to scratches up Sheila's driver side window trying to get her out while grawling at her. With Sam being bold enough to open the front door and take a shot at it the creature just stood there gazing at Sam before it would take a step forward towards Sam "Get the heck!! away from her!!" said Sam. As the creature started to backing up going the other way while grawling at both Sam and Sheila. Knowning for sam and family this isn't over but the beginning of a long fight. Suddenly the creature camouflage itself to do the unthinkable it did that to get Sheila outta the car but instead it went up on the porch and strike Sam on the arm with it's powerful talons leaving a 2" laceration that made Sam weak. As Sheila screams as Sheila watches her father fall on the porch. Jon came a running and shooting at the creature. Which turned invisible but you can hear it breathe with a unsual scent.

Looking down Jon had to hit it. Because it's bleeding an orange like not red for some reason. As the creature bleeds on the side of the house on it's way back to the tracks Jon took it upon himself to follow it and see where is it going.

But it disappeared on him. As Jon heads back to the house to check with his dad and sister as nearby neighbors came to assist the Bentford's. Because of gun shots were heard for someone had call the Sheriff's office to report it. But Jon returned to the house and knowning that the creature will returned again but don't know when but Jon will also be ready for it. "Dad! Sheila! Are you both alright?" ask Jon while they hug each other: for comfort. "What in the heck!

Was that thing!?" ask Sheila. "We are still trying to figured it out ourselves and no we don't know what that is." said Jon. "We know it came here to kill us." said Sam. As picking Sam up off of the front porch where the creature had knock him down and left Sam cut bad from the creature's talons. said Sheila "well we did come face to face with it."

"But for sure I know with all my heart that darn thing will come back here again you can count on it." said Jon. "He is going to get one of us for sure next time." said Sam. "What does it want!?" ask Sheila. "Heck! Sheila! We don't know why it's here or what it wants it just targeting us for some apparent reason." said Jon. "But when I shot it it bled a unusual color of orange so this is no ordinary alien." said Jon. "What we need to do is be prepared when it does returned." said Jon. "I Can't believe this!" said Sam. "What's that dad?" ask Jon. "Hear we are fighting some dam creature from another time of some." said Sam. "And it has it's own train it makes you think what times we are living in." said Sam. As the Bentford's started walking into the house, Sheriff Protzman and one of his deputy decided to pull up in front of the house to go and question the Bentford's about the shooting that someone had called in on.

But the Bentford's kept quiet on the rights not to say a word about the creature and told them what they wanted to hear instead. "Hey sheriff what can we do for you?" ask Jon.

"Well one of your neighbor's called and said that there was shots coming from your residences." "so can you explained to me Jon?"ask the sheriff. While Sam and Sheila are sitting on the sofa observing at what was said as the deputy was being nosey as usual he founded a orange substance near the porch where the creature was shot at. "Sheriff! You might wanted see this." said the deputy. "What is that?" ask the Sheriff. "It looks to me like this is some type of dna." said the deputy. "So Jon! Come here." said the Sheriff. "Yes sir sheriff." said jon. "Again explained to me why were there shots?" ask the sheriff. "I thought I heard a bear on the front porch so I shot off one." said Jon. "A bear was on your porch?" Ask the deputy. As both sheriff and the deputy look at one another. For one there aren't any wild in the area and all sense no one has reported seeing any ferocious and dangerous animals in the metropolitan area. So what Jon is saying doesn't make one bit of sense to both deputy and the sheriff. "Well you just don't shoot a bear and orange dna runs out of it." said the deputy. "Sheriff! I know what I saw on our porch!" said Jon. "Ok son." said the Sheriff. "But you just said you heard a bear not saw a bear so which is it? Jon! Ask the sheriff. "We are just trying to get the facts here." said the sheriff. "Ok Jon so where is the carcase of the bear you shot?" ask the sheriff. In reality the sheriff knows something is so unperculiar about this incident: that just doesn't sit well with him.

Now by the time that the sheriff has quiz Jon enough. Sam intervene on his son's behalf to keep things to a level. "Say sheriff why are you trying to make a big deal out of all of this s—t! when you need to find the responsible one that kidnap my wife or murdered her!" huh!? Ask Sam. But you come here and ask my son about a damn bear! What in the hell is wrong with you?" ask Sam. "I'am so sorry Sam I know that you all are still grieving over June's absence we will let you all be to yourselves so goodnight to you all." said the sheriff. As Sam stood there in a emotional stake watching the sheriff leave. As both Jon and Sheila come to comfort there dad at a horrible moment when thinking about Mrs. June Bentford. Who was the center piece of there lives.

She has being gone for six months or more and Sam believes that this creature has something to do with her absence.

So that's why Sam and Jon wants to finish the job them selves. But not just for June's sake. But for all that was in the wake of death with this creature. Now that this creature has expose itself to the Bentford's and vice versa so this need ed to be finished soon or later. As the family makes preparation in to destroying the locomotive with the creature on it. But least jon did wound it so now the creature itself will want some type of retribution for wounding it. So the family will be the main target until everyone is wipeout or the creature is dead itself.

As both Jon and Sheila walks towards the backyard they can see where the creature had it's d.n.a track to the railroads as Jon and his sister had followed to see which way did it go last night. It went far as the track bed and then disappear.

Both Jon and Sheila can look and see a locomotive engine headed towards them at top speed so Jon and Sheila went to hide themselves in the tall stocks of corn to get out of the presence of the creature and to see if the engine will stop.

"I hope this is it." said Jon. Whispering to his sister. "Jonny blow it head off." said Sheila. Whispering back at her brother. But both was a little disappointed because that engine kept going with boxcars filled with freights moving and pulling with power. "Shuck's! I was ready again to pump one more into it head." said Jon. "But for all I care is it might be somewhere bleeding to death. Now the next move is the creature's. And it strikes again in a unusual way. But it gets it's prey unexpectedly In a cleaver and smooth way to get it's prey out of the house.

A Idle Locomotive

Chpt VII

Now it's being days since Sheila has with her father and brother until her husband Jay is wandering why his wife has being gone for days. So he decides to show up over at the in laws house full of curiousity: Why Sheila hasn't come home like she must. So jay came in asking his wife "Hey Sheila what in the heck! Is going on here!?" asking Jay. "I being up all night and day thinking what in the world happen to my wife?" said Jay. "Honey I need you home." said Jay. Now as big brother Jon intervene on his sister 's part to where Jon and Jay both got into a little argument over Sheila's whereabouts. But Sam had to shut up both Jon and Jay from all that nonsense. While Sheila runs into her old bedroom and shut the door behind her for to clear her head.

In the kitchen Sam bring Jay in and sit him down to explain what is really going on. Sam told Jay somethings but Jay just looks at Sam with a I don't understand look. So Sam tells Jay to go home and let Sheila be. But Jay refuses to go alone he wants his wife to come home with him. So Jay is not leaving without his wife as he makes it clear with the in laws. "Well suit yourself." said Sam. As Sam and Jon get ready to run to the store to get a bit of grocery for the house that leaves Sheila and husband Jay there at the house. Which could be a bit dangerous but Jay will sorted of protect his wife. Because Sheila was in the bed taking a nap when her father and brother left for the store. But she didn't know that Jay was still in the house with her. Now the creature is coming back to get his prey. As it parks it engine down the track ways off. But it left the engine running to you can still hear it. As it steps down off the engine into the side of the track bed to camouflage itself once again for to strike and grab it prey and go.Now getting close to the Bentford's house thru the backyard from the corn field. As it stop to gazes at the house to see if there is any movement. And yes it found Jay sitting in the kitchen at the table snacking on some cracker and sipping on a cold beer. While Jay is enjoying his beer and cracker. He heard a bump up against the house but thought nothing of it. This time the noise was up above him until Sheila heard it to from in the other room.

Sheila came running out of her old bedroom yelling for her dad and brother but all she gotten was her husband. "Sheila your dad and brother went to the grocery store they be back momentarily." said Jay. "Honey! What's a matter!?" asking Jay. "I heard a noise coming from the roof!" said Sheila. "I heard it a minute ago I thought maybe it's your dad and Jon back already." said Jay. And sheila looks out in the driveway to see if her father's truck returned. "Dad's truck is not out there." said Sheila."Well I can go and see what transpired on the roof." said Jay. As Sheila yells at him "Nooo ooooo! Don't you dare open the door and go nowhere!" said Sheila. But Jay was trying to show how much of a man he is by checking it out. But also Sheila was begging for him not to go but he insist on going to see what's on the roof of the house. To check out that strange bumping on the roof of the house. And it dark out back and no lights nowhere to see unless you have a strong flashlight. The second Jay open the back door there was a strong odour near the door that Sheila she had smelt before. As Jay put one foot on the back porch the creature stabs Jay in the chest with it sharp talons then place Jay over it's shoulder then left grawling loud. While Sheila fainted from what she just saw at what had happen to her husband. Now the creature has another victim that shouldn't died in vain.As the creature makes a getaway with Jay in hand. Sam and Jon are pulling up into the driveway as both Sam and Jon reaches the porch they heard that engine sound of a train coming near the house. Sam and Jon both rushes into the house and finds Sheila on the floor and the back door wide opened.

With blood on the porch. "Sheila! Honey! Sheila! Wake up!" said Sam. "Where is Jay!?" asking Jon. As she started crying. "The monster took him!" said Sheila. Jon went out the back and went far as the corn field yelling Jay's name. "Jay! Jay!" said Jon. But all he received was his own echo. As returning to the house Jon came into the house asking his sister "Sheila what happened!?" asking Jon.

Now as Sheila explaines at what had happen Jon is now full of fury hate and anger towards this creature. "we need some explosive."said Jon. "Jonny! C'mon now we can't jeopardize everyone else around us." said Sam. "Well! Dad! What are we going to do!?" asking Jon. "It took mom as you claim and now it has Jay!" said Jon. "So again! What are we going to do to takeout this sucker ass!? Asked Jon. "Because i'am tired of playing around with this(expletive) bastard of a creat ure!" said Jon."Jonny! Come and help your sister up."said Sam. "Now we don't want to rush in without a strategy son and you know that." said Sam. "I'am just ready to get this creature's but so bad I can taste it." said Jon. "It's a ugly thing to not look at and tall with ugly paws and long talons." said Sheila. "And it has my husband too." said Sheila. With anger in her voice while crying. Therefore the family needs to focus and stick together with all steadfast and humble ness. Meanwhile the creature has struck again and made it successfully with an easy prey to feast on.

Soon the creature would've got so desperate to feed it will started to loose all of it capabilties when going after it's prey. It has special skills in visiability leaping and defy gravity and move object's with a gaze. So this creature is a hybrid of a bigfoot and a center for a basketball team.

But having killing instincts is another part of it's nature and habits from evil developing over time. More like a dog when it's a pup it doesn't know any better until it becomes an adult dog it will bite all day long. That's it's nature and habit.

But this creature doesn't know anything about being good because nothing has shown it anything about having good in it's character. All it knows is evil all it knows is to kill what it's going to eat. Before it would rip it prey open it does a small ritual before it would eat anything. That is to remove it's preys legs to keep it from running and remove it other limbs so it can't defend itself. So it's need it's prey very helpless as possible. Therefore this creature's cleaverness is so great it does respects the engine by not eating on it. It's drags it's prey off of the engine in a tunnel and finish it there with the remaines on the side of the track bed. The engine is more like the sanctuary in which evil dwells upon it. If the creature is ever expose to a human being then the human must die. Because the creature doesn't like being looked upon and then target. So it get it's prey before it' prey will target it.

Meanwhile back at the Bentford's place. Sheila is in a bit of a rage cause Jay sacrifice his life for hers in which was so stupid on Jay's part. And Sheila wants her father to report at what happen to her husband to the authority. But Sam is trying not to go to the authorities Sam and Jon want to dealt with this creature on their own terms with great satisfaction afterwards with also abundance of joy at hand for the ones in spirit. Both Sam and Jon knows with all their hearts that it will be back soon enough. For another victim like Sheila a easy target and not know way harmful but helpless cause of being a female human is as vulnerable for an attack if not careful. But the Bentford's knows how cleaver this creature is and now no more chances it's getting.

So Sam and Jon both have a bit of an ideal with just a handful of special supplies with Sheila's help also can come in hand. So each of the Bentford's knows what to do on their part at getting rid of this thorn in their side for good. But only one thing that come to mind of each one is. When is that killer of a creature shall returned? Is the question. All they know is to be prepared and wait on it. So both Sam and Jon go out at the same time different days looking up and down the tracks for a sitting engine to run upon the creature and catching it off guard. They know that Jay is presume to be dead an which they know ain't a thing can be done about it. But to have the head of this creature exploded by sending it to kingdom come. As all three of the Bentford's leaving to go and do their normal search for the days end. Speeding away from the house going north towards the tracks to look and check for that sitting engine But Ed Sam's bestfriend from grade school had passed the family in the opposite direction going south.

But Ed decides to turn his vehicle around and follow the Bentford's to see what they are up to. But he stay back about two hundred feet so they can't notice him following them. With Sam driving like a bat outta hell it's no wonder if he doesn't get pull over but the family is on a mission to stop a killer from doing what it knows best.

As the Bentford's ride for miles along the state tracks to find the killer is in a days work. But they hasn't notice Ed is tailing them for an hour. As Sam pulls into a gas station to get more fuel into the truck for tomorrow drive and grab a twelve pack of beer and Sheila and Jon both wanted a hot dog and a bottle of soda of any kind. While both Sheila and Jon sat in the truck until Sam returns. Sheila notice that Ed's car was parked on the other side of the store lot with him inside of it watching them from a distance. So waiting on their father's to returned to the truck to let him know of Ed's watching them and not quite sure if he's following them or not.

As Jon gets out to help his father by pumping the gas for him then Sheila decides to get out and scretches her long legs while doing so Sheila ask her father was that Ed's car over there with him inside? Sam was looking to see if that was him and quite sure it was him. As Sam started to walk over to see what his old friend was up to. When Sam got closer to the car Ed started to act nerves for some reason.

"Hey Ed! What are you doing here?" ask Sam. "Well I was waiting on someone to meet me here but it's looks like I was stood up again." said Ed.

"Wait a minute here Why are you and the kids driving this far out?" ask Ed. "Well like you we was also stood up to." said Sam.

As Sam tried so hard to not to spill the beans. By keeping the family secrets out of harms way. But soon or later the cat does happens to get out of the bag some how. But to Ed he knows better then that Ed knows that this family is hiding something and he is trying to discover it. Or maybe help. Because in Ed's head ain't one family in all of Lajunta area has that many weapon's to display in their home. So he waits for the Bentford's to leave first so he can followed them back to their area. And Sam notice that Ed is tailing them for some dam reason.So Sam pulls over to the side of the road to see why is Ed tailing them. "Hey Ed why in the heck are you tailing us?" ask Sam. "Ok. I seen you all speeding from your house and then I thought you had heard something about June's whereabouts." said ed. "So I said oh what the hell and followed you." said Ed. "Ed! Go home and I will call you later and explain to you at what's going on." ok? Ask Sam. "Sammy. Call me. I wants to help." said Ed. "I will call you." said Sam. So Sam went and got back into his truck and pull off. Looking back into his rear view mirror to see what Ed is determining to do.

But sat there until the bentford's got outta sight. Then Ed took off speeding to determines to see what is going on with his oldest and dear friend in the world had Ed so darn curious about what is happening. So Ed refuses to back off trying his best to get more more involved.

Finally Ed caught up with the Bentford's and trying not to be spotted by the family in no formal shape or fashion way ever. Keeping his distance and trying to remained calm at whatever transpired or happen. As Ed watches closely at the way Sam's driving patterns when coming to all railroad crossing's. Sam some how slowly stops and looks up the tracks before going on across. As Ed do the same wandering what are they looking for? As Ed asking himself. Now arriving back home the Bentford's all get out of the truck and check around the house for any unusual things. In which the air smelt a little funny to all three. "Dad it's being here and gone."saidJjon. "I smell it too."said Sam. "the night it took Jay that's what I smelt."said Sheila. Standing on the side of the house looking for any danger or harm to the house. The Bentford's saw Ed driving by. Because Ed has to pass the Bentford's home to get to his home. But ed just looks strait ahead. By trying not to know what this family is up to. Ed acting like he was minding his own business but still a very nosey friend. As Sam thought.

The Boxcar of Silence

Chpt VIII

The next day it rain like it hasn't rain in a year or two.But also cold out. The rain was coming out of the mountains to causes the weather to change tremendously down in the valley all around the Rio Grande area.But doesn't slow the plans down for the Bentford's mission to catch and kill a monster that kills and terrorized the family to eat. But to the bentford's not another meal it's getting. As walking into the kitchen Sheila notice there was a boxcar sitting alone over the way as she thought of grabbing the umberella and take a look to see what inside of that boxcar.

But started to pour down pretty hard to you couldn't see out.

"Good morning sweetie." said Sam. But no reply from shelia as she stood gazing at the boxcar wiping away tears of sadness thinking of her husband Jay. As Sam comes over to her and show comfort to her. "Dad I really miss Jay and he was my precious heart."said Sheila. "Honey we will get this so call bigfoot having creature ass." said Sam. "For Jay and June sake." said Sam. "Morning What's for breakfast?" ask Jon."What's wrong?"asking Jon. "Your sister just misses her Jay so much." said Sam. "Is that a boxcar sitting?" asking Jon. Jon open the back door and went to the edge of the porch while the rain just pouring down. As he was doing the same like Sheila was thinking of her husband Jon other wise thought of his mother while looking as the rain kept coming down. But before Jon thought about coming back into the house he gaze for awhile at thee boxcar the way.

Wandering so much at what's inside of that boxcar. In which the curiousity does have the cats attention but also kills it.

As the rain starts to let up a bit Jon was thinking of a walk over to that boxcar so Jon yells into the house to let his dad and sister know that he is taking a walk over to the tracks. "So do y'all wants to go also?" ask Jon. "Well yeah we all should go together I think."said Sheila. As Sam grabs one of his rifle for protection just in case something might jump off.

Sam is ready to lay someone down when it comes to his children. Jon and Sheila is all he have now. So he is no way taking any chances on loosing his children. He lost his wife which is a devastating lost with a son in law gone now is a tragic lost to Sheila the most. And loosing a love one is a very hard thing to accept. But to the Bentford's no acceptance is needed. But indeed their minds are set for revenge on the creature that is so much in responsibility that took everything from them. So killing it would be just right for everyone's needs. The creature didn't care if it took June's &

Jay and others lives. All it cares about is another meal and where is it coming from. So you can understand this family attitude towards this creature.

With everyday about living without a love ones presence can bare pressure for hatred. When nothing is being done about the situation. So Sheila and her father are a tightly knitted family along with Jon as the true protector. Now as the family of three has the guts to walk to check this big boxcar to see what's on it. As the Bentford's make a scrimmage line going towards the boxcar so if any movement shoot first then ask questions later. Because no chances with this thang. "I'am getting the creeps if I see this thang shucks!" said Sheila. Jon covers one side and Sam down the other while Sheila kept her eyes up and down the tracks looking for on coming engines. Jon calls his dad to come on the otherside of the boxcar to get the door to slide back which he needs help sliding the door back. As both Jon and Sam saw something that was devastating shameful and no love for what they seen. A boxcar full of human remaines and the odour was so awful and undepicable to both Jon and Sam had to regurgitate from the smell of it. "Dad! Remember when I ask you before what are we going to do?" ask Jon.

"Yeah I remember son." said Sam. "Well what are the (explicit)we going to do?" Jon asking in anger. "We stick to the plans son." said Sam. As Sheila comes around the boxcar to see what her brother and father were looking at. "Sheila!

Don't come any further or you gonna wish you wouldn't." said Sam. So Sheila stops in her tracks cause she can smell the smell from where she is standing. "I'am going to be sick!" said Sheila. (coughing).

As both Sam and Jon was getting off the boxcar. Sam looks down in the doorway of the boxcar and found a pentdant that looks so familiar like the one he bought June for her birthday five year earlier. If there is a engraving on the back of it. It's June's. Sam turns it over to see if his and hers initials are on the back. And Sam right away started hollering at the top of his voice. "Dad!! what's wrong!!"asking Sheila.

"I found something that belongs to your mother!" said Sam.

"This is mom's pentdant you bought for her on her birthday." said Sheila. "I want that (explicit) creature's ass for sure now!" said Sam. "Dad do you think mom's corpes is among all that in this boxcar?" asking Jon. "Well son ain't no telling." said Sam. "So this creature did have something to do with June's disappearance and death." said Sam. "This thang took mom away from us?" ask Sheila. As she stood there in tears wandering why this thang wanted with her mother.

And Sam couldn't no longer bare the site and smell of the boxcar and what was on it. "C'mon kids I had enough for one day." said Sam. As walking back to the house Sam kept looking at his precious wife's pentdant thinking and wishing she was walking beside him right about now. But bearing the pain just looking at it so much. To where Sam questioning himself "If I just would've stayed home that day June would probably be here beside me." the thought of Sam. By walking back towards the house everyone stop to look at each other because of that particular sound of a on coming engine from the west end of the tracks.

As the family takes off running to the house as fast as they can to get there weapons and be on point for destruction is coming. By all means do or die. To the Bentford's no one is lying down today for all rights to live life intentionally is to shoot and kill on sight. But the Bentford's knows this thang quite well to catch it in a snare. It's capabilties are a disadvantage to the defending family but all of nothing for a small war that shouldn't happen but a small price was paid with their lives taken. So an eye for an eye life for a life. The thought of the Bentford's.

What a lousy disappointment. The four locomotive's was pulling freight behind it and speeding pulling with power.

Didn't stop for nothing. And nothing better not get in it's way. And the Bentford's all stood on the back porch there and ready for whatsoever come let it come. And now Jon starts to lose his cool over the matter that this creature is a nuisance and a thorne in the side. But while standing on the porch Sheila notice that the barn door is wide open for some reason the door seems to be off of it's hinges. "Why is the barn door looking like it is?" ask Sheila. "That muth-(explicit) got into the barn now i'm going to kill it for sure!" said Sam. As walking to the barn slowly and cautious. Jon lead the way with his mossberg 500 shotgun which wasn't a joke. With

Jon's aiming for the right target can annihilate the object. Now at the barn door they go inside slow and very careful looking around for something that may look unfamiliar that shouldn't be there. "Sheila dad! You both notice somethin?" ask Jon. "Only thing I notices is that smell is in here." said Sheila. "My point exactly." said Jon.

Right away the Bentford's was looking for this creature to jump out in the moment. By covering the whole barn the Bentford's was again unlucky to come up with nothing.

And knowing the creature's scent is a alarming way to knowning it's whereabouts and coming's. But only one weakness there is that no one can see invisible beings when you are prey upon. Being terrorized by this creature is something strange the Bentford's and others has to be alert at all time.

But true enough the family hasn't seen this much fun in hunting for a ugly smelling hairy red eyes big paws long talons having creature. When you think you got the world by the balls that's when the stuff hits you hard. As looking over the way that boxcar that was full of corpse remaines is gone. But which way did it go? Is the question. The Bentford's were covering the barn at that time to see what was inside since the creature decides to destroyed the small barn door. Like a stanky maniac at large.

Once again that creature of a devil got away again. Without anyone knowning it. "(Explicit) that bastard came and got that boxcar and left." said Sam. "Did one of you hear it coming?" "Because I didn't hear a thing." said Sam. "Dad we didn't hear a thing neither." said Jon. Then suddenly a loud crash to see the creature at work again. As that locomotive plows into a box truck in the crossing's. As the Benford's watches quietly to see what is about to transpired in front of then over the way. The driver was decease from the looks of things. "Are you kidding me?" ask Jon. "Dad let's nail this stanky ass bastard now." said Jon. "What the (explicit) are we waiting on?" ask Jon.

As both Sam and Sheila stayed quiet while looking on. But Jon show to much excitement to get it over with. While the truck was on fire they saw the creature use it power to put the flames out. Then retrieved the dead and burn victim.

"Hey. Did you see what it just did?" ask Sam. (whispering).

Then it move the once burning truck to the side of the track bed by gazing at it. "That is crazy did you see what in the (explicit) it did?" said Jon. As the creature aboard the engine with another victim making it casualty number until they lost count. "Dad! What are we going to do? Just let that (explicit) going about it business!"said Jon."Wait one damn minute son!" didn't you see what the thang did out there?" ask Sam. "So what! We suppose to be impressed because all the tricks it did?" ask Jon. "Son be patient calm down I know you wants this bastards as well as I do too."said Sam.

So let's work together and stick to the plans." Ok? Ask Sam.

"Sorry dad I just get so excited until I wants to shoot something." said Jon"Well soon enough you will get the opportunity to do so."said Sam. "Actually all three of us would love to shoot this thang from hell."said Sam. "Believe me kids we are going to get some justice out of this situation." said Sam. "Believe what I say to you is getting my revenge is sweet to me because that thang took my wife your mother and Jay so killing that thang would bring me all so pleasure." said Sam.

As Sam mentioning Jay's name has brought tears to his daughter Sheila's eyes."Sorry. Honey I still know that you truely misses him. "Why are family it's targeting?" ask Sheila, (in a emotional stake)."I wish I knew."said Sam. Then and there it hit sam suddenly "Wait a moment Your mother had to seen this thang from the time I last saw and talk with her until she had left the house to go and get stuff for the pantry for the church and then June went the direction of the tracks and that thang was waiting on her to cross." said Sam. (Explicit)!! it did kill June! The thought of Sam.

"We need to find that locomotive if the locomotive is spotted then that's where it will be." said Sam. "But dad it can be anywhere in the whole tri county area." said Jon."I don't care where it's at we need to catch it and kill it." said sam.

"I was hoping that it would come back here so we can fight it on our own turf." said Sam. As the saying go's be careful for what you ask for Because it may just happen the way you ask for. Never talk the talk unless you experience the walk. But the Bentford's has experience the walk with the talk to backup their brush against death at their own back door. With that being said the creature is going to strike again for to eliminate the whole family if necessary. But not able to. The Bentford's are as hard as they come and the creature must understand that. Now the Bentford's are on their porch standing there talking about having other families that was victimize from this creature to put on a memorial benefit at the town's square in two months. For the missing love ones and ones died from an accident's at the tracks some how but couldn't prove nothing ever happen. So they became missing.

With many feet from the Bentford's home are some tall trees over the way which grew over the years. Is a haven for birds of all wildlife. But for weeks those trees have become a aid to the creature's being. It uses the trees to camouflage itself from it's prey and to look down also on it's prey from a distance. As high up it can see with deceptive vision as if a bird can do also.

While looking in on it's main target it's trying to decide who and when to attack. As it grawls to itself looking on the target jumping down to walk back to it's engine sitting on the second set of tracks down ways from the Bentford's home.

Waiting and watching for a meal to come which it also knows it's a determination to eat but a fight that can go both ways lose or win live or die. Only time will tell with a beast going up against man. But the one with the very best strategy is the one that is reign superior. The Heavenly creator did not intentionally wanted beast of the earth to topple man to reign on earth. But some beast are in fury to man.

In which the man becomes the hunted one. Or the bottom of the food chain in that case it will never happen: as long as the beasts mind stay the same. Can't think for itself and without a conscience then it's just an ordinary animal that rely on humans to do and think for it.

And as for a new born baby is the same to where the baby depends on it's parent's to feed and to correct it's diaper's when needed. But the little that people would know is that this creature use to be a man of evil and wicked ways until it became cursed from it's natural behavior of killing and stealing other humans and then became a cannibal from eating others. It made a transfiguration over a period of time for doing what it was doing. So this creature was born a good and decent human full of integrity and strong mind to be a train engineer but was done wrong in the past until he was fed up with life's offers. And didn't want no part of it.

Then the transfiguration had carry weight of hatred for all mankind and with this came slowly with a very hairy body finger nails grew into talons his hands turned to paws the height of it stature grew tremendously and it's eyes are red from evil and wicked to where both dwell inside. And with that terroritory comes the special powers that allowed the creature to do what it's need to do to survive.

Signals of Destruction
Chpt IX

The next day the rails were busy then ever. But no signs of the engine forty three eleven and neither the creature. But the day was also cold with a touch of sun. As all three of the Bentford's decided to make a quick run to the store for abundances of items for the house. But as leaving the house the sheriff and the deputy pull up to check on the family to see if they needed anything. But no one said anything regards to the creature.

"Sam I stop to see how you all are holding up I didn't mean to prior in on you all if you are busy." said the sheriff.

"Well we are doing the best that we can without June's presences." said Sam. "Ok Sam being truthful with you we haven't come close to solve June's disappearance I know that there is more to her situation." said the sheriff. "But we don't have much to go on." said the sheriff. "Look we need a few more weeks to go on. All we got is a missing persons to go on. "Well gene you do what you have to do." said Sam. "What do you mean by that?" ask the sheriff.

"I mean if you are looking for evidents then do so." said Sam. "I hope the law finds him before I do that's what i'am getting at." said Sam. Then Sam walks away mumbling to himself more less calling the sheriff and the deputy worthless and poethic (Explicit). It's ashamed that some can solve a crime quicker then the local authorities who is just wasted tax payer money on just one crime alone. So that's why Sam and his two children needed to keep this under the radar as long as possible. To the Bentford's they don't need no authorities involved whatsoever. Sam made that clear with his son Jon not to tell a soul. Sam wants this creature just as bad as the creature wants them. A fight to the fullest have every bit to a finished. Like a boxing match the fighter's can't wait to opposed his opponent in the ring to settle all or nothing with the winner's hand raised. And the loser's have concieve but not content to how the fight went.

As backing out of the driveway Sam ask both Jon & Sheila if he was doing the right thing from with holding information from the Sheriff? But both Jon & Sheila took their dad's side of things. With a better way of thinking then to share information with someone who doesn't care about the situation. Out of all the talk the family was suddenly silent when they came to the tracks because the signals were flashing the gates were down also. But no train insight.

"Shucks! Where are you?" asking in thought Sam. Now Jon gets out to take a look up and down the track. But again no train whatsoever. So Jon returned to get back into the truck to take off. A minute to soon the whole family would have died. Because the minute it took for Jon to return to the truck and with a speeding on coming locomotive would have determine the fate of the Bentford's(Explicit)! said Sam. With four locomotive's pulling the freight behind it means the freight was very heavy and nothing can't be in the way of all the ton's of steel. Unless their destiny is to die. As Sam was sitting in the passenger's seat gazing at the flashing red signals and thinking how close death was at their disposal again. But once the train has pass through the Bentford's wasn't press for time but was content to harm a dangerous creature without any signals. Just destroyed vs destruction human vs beast and predator vs victims.

As the Bentford's stay focus on their everyday life and not on the creature soon enough it would come out of hiding and then strike when unexpected. Then the signals of destruction will not work for a killer's perpective but works on lovin life. And the Bentford's did love life at all angles.

While in hiding like a crook that stole from life's humble and need one more piece the creature is getting his red eyes full of the Bentford's home. And when they leave when they returned home. So it's very clever when it's hungry intellegent when it want to kill. Again once was a smart man before becoming of a wicked creature. Without a conscience and no love within the nature of it is unstable and dangerous to fight against for pound vs power the creautre would defeat it's prey. But in strategy of the human mind and tho ught's will prevailed at the end.

As riding through the town on Hartford road Sam glance up one set of railroad tracks and saw a black on red engine just sitting idle as always. So Sam asking Jon to pull over to the next lot. "Sheila I need for you to stay here in the truck." said Sam. "Son you walk with me." said Sam. Jon and Sam both grab their hardware for protection. From this unpredictable half man half creature. In the back of Sam's mind is this the day for a small war to end. Or is this the day for him and his son to die also. Walking up the tracks quickly and in a hurry to catch this culprit in his skin. "Jonny! You take the otherside and I got this side." said Sam. As Sam ease up the steps of the engine to the door with Jon covering the other door the two gentlemen that was inside one was reading a book while the other was reading a local newspapaer.

Sam tapped the window of the engine with his rifle and both men were afraid to open the doors of the engine. Then one of the guy's decides to come out of the cab of the engine to see what Sam needed. But Sam gradually apologize for frightening the men. "We are so sorry we are looking for somebody else." said Sam. "Well who are you both looking for?" ask the gentleman. "Well you guy's wouldn't understand c'mon Jonny!"said sam.(Explicit)!! I thought this was that thang hanging around throughout the town." said Sam."Dad that was close in killing someone else." said Jon.

Sam did the right thing in checking the cab of the engine before shooting first. If not both Sam and Jon would've be responsible in killing two innocent bystanders for mistaken identity. But it seen that the creature is now playing with the Bentford's mind. As Jon again starting to loose his cool in this whole ordeal. "It seem that we aren't getting anywhere with this (Explicit) thang."said Jon. "Son will you calm down now dammit! We are getting real close in catching this thang so don't freak out on me now." said Sam. As both men headed back to the truck and take off. "Well was that the thang? Or did you both get it?" ask Sheila. "Honey, I wish it was but no it wasn't it it was two guys and boyee was they scared of us."said Sam. (laughing). Now the sun is starting to go down and the air turned cold so winter is not far from coming into play soon enough. The Bentford's arrived at the market as Jon stay with the truck while Sheila and Sam go into the store to grab items for the house so Sheila can cook dinner for the evening. And the Bentford's was trying to be back at home before the fall of night. To be inside just in case it decides to show up for a fight. Forty five minutes later both Sam and Sheila coming out of the market with two not one shopping cart two full of grocerie's. "Wow! Did you both buy up the whole darn store?" ask Jon.

"Do you remember we are out about of eveything?" said Sheila. "Let's hurry you both." said Sam. As both Jon and Sheila put the groceries in the back of the truck so it want make a mess when Jon turn the corners. "Man! What a day." said Sam. "And my arm starts to hurt where that creature cut me with it's talons I can still feel that pain." said Sam. "When we catch it i'am going to put a bunch of hole in it's carcase." said Sam. Almost home as coming to those tracks again Jon steps out to take a caution look to see if that locomotive is near or insight. But the engine isn't there but the creature it's around to strike in the moment. As Jon pulls into the driveway of the house it's awfully dark on the country roads at night. While Sheila get the door both sam and Jon started bring in the grocerie's but while Jon was on the back of the truck he heard a branch split in the tree in the front yard over the driveway. As Jon ease to the cab of the truck to grab his double barrel shot gun to shoot at whatsoever is up in the tree then Sam return to the truck looking at Jon and his movement to Sam did the same by grabbing his rifle and now both men surrounding the tree looking up into the tree to see what is going on.

"I heard a branch or a limb snap. Like something is in this tree." said Jon. "It could be that damn thang again." said Sam. "Dad I don't know but it's up there." said Jon. Then Sheila had come out of the house looking to see what's going on. "Dad! Jonny! It's that thang again!" "How do you know?!"ask Jon. "Can you both smell that?!" ask Sheila. The minute Sheila said that. Hear it comes out of the tree it come jumping down fighting with both men knocking Jon's gun out of his hands and slice Sam's arm again with it's talons.

As it went in circles around to get Jon for itself grawling with anger to get what it want. But Jon kept kicking at it.

Until Sam had enough strength to let a shot off into the creature's leg and it started bleeding with orange substance running out of it. As the Bentford's wounded the creature's body the second time. It's comes back with a vengence like a monster with a vendetta you hurt me I hurt you. Now as the creature take off running again to it's engine for a quick recovery. But Jon was running in back of it to put one more slug into it's body but Jon misses and hit at the side of the barn. "You muth(Explicit)! Come back for some more you piece of crap!" said Jon. "I can't believe I missed that piece of (Explicit)!" said Jon. As Jon returned to see if his dad and sister was ok helping his dad get up from the ground into the house. But they can see the light on the engine to where the creature was backing up going into the opposite direction from the house.

"Jonny did you get it?"ask Sam."No dad I missed it." said Jon."Now you know it's going to return for some more figthing until it can get one of us." said Sam. "Well dad like you said before we must be ready at all times." said Jon.

"Right?" ask Jon. "That's it son." said Sam. When the creature escape again it left quite a bit of it's dna in the front yard an along the side of the house. But like before the next day it's dna wasn't there. Like it disappears in the sun.

For some reason the creature's dna is green but when it hit's the air the oxygen turns it orange in which makes it so perculiar. As Jon steps into the middle of the yard where him and the creature were fighting and retrieve it's dna in a jar to study it further more. "Would you look at this (Explicit)." said Jon. "You can see how potent it's dna is." said Jon.

"Jonny don't waste that(Explicit) on my kitchen floor please sir." said Sam. "Jonny you better be careful with that stuff cause you don't know what's in that." said Sheila. As Jon scoops up more of the creature's dna to examined it for a study. But Jon knows several people at the university of colorado that wouldn't mind taking a look at a sample of a mysterious life forum. But may required a little time and also monetary to do so. As the next day came about Sam needed to go to see his doctor for a technical shot for those deep cut laceration's on his right fore arm. Which was very bad for a man his age to go about and ignore the pain.

So Sheila saw to it that Sam made it to the doctor's office to have his arm looked at and also his health too. Sam got up this morning complaining about being lightheaded just a bit. And not knowning signs and symptoms that he needs to beware of. In how close Sam's health starts to deteriorate in lack of not taking care of himself since June's disappearance Sam hasn't being the same. He hardly eats much and down a beer before breakfast and working on automobile's while smoking two packs a day. So Sam's health is not what it use to be when his June was around. June would make Sam brush his teeth before going to work and supper too afterwards. Sam's sight starts to get bad from not watching what he do eat sometime. But Sam do love a good pork chops with biscuits and gravy. And when June was there she would make a very descent breakfast for sam and the kids.

Like grits and sausage or blueberry waffles with home fries and that's what they all missed about not having Mrs. June around. Now Sam expected Sheila would pickup where June has left off in cooking for him and Jon. Not having Mrs. Bentford around does anger Sam a lot that would cause him to give up so easy. But his children's love for him is what keeps him going among other things. But while Sheila and Sam left the house to go to the doctor's office to get his arm looked at and also his health as well. But Sam is quite worried about what his physician may see or tell him.

As Sheila convinces her father that things would be alright for him so to stop worrying. But Sam always had June as his mouthpiece Sam wouldn't tell the doctor all what was wrong with him June would. Because she didn't wanna see her husband of many years in pain at all. But once inside of the clinic Sam felt some relieve cause there was many men his age was there also get looked at. For what Sam can see is that many of those men that are there have several issues with their own health. "I hope your brother will be ok at the house by himself." said Sam. "Now you know dad that Jonny is going to be Jonny." said Sheila.

Therefore at the house Jon was getting prepared to leave for a moment with that jar of orange goop from the creature's body and head over to the university for someone can take a look at it. But Jon looks out the back door and saw the locomotive with a boxcar attached to it so Jon went and grab his weapon immediately for another round of fighting alone with this creature. By the time Jon came back to the back door the locomotive was slowly pulling off going westbound. And Jon just stood there watching the engine as it gets out of sight before he leave the house. Just to be sure that nothing was going to harm him or the house. So leaving the house Jon made sure that nothing is getting into the house but the outside was pretty much out of his control if the creature would comes back again it needs to feed on a human and not a empty house. But as Jon leaves he passes Ed going in the opposite direction why Ed started to stop but no vehicles were in the driveway so Ed kept going on about his business. Why Jon didn't even look Ed's way Jon just kept his head strait.

Now Sam is about to go into the room to have his body to be examined and to have all his vidal's check and as his doctor enter the room "Hi i'am Doctor Letchell can you enligthing me About what's going on?" and what did you do to your arm?" ask Doctor Letchell. "Well I damage it in my barn." said Sam. While Sheila just gazed at him for telling the physician a lie. Sheila came over and stood next to her father so she can whisper into his ear. About lying to the doctor. "If you don't tell the truth I will." said Sheila. As she gave her father the look. "Ok doc. I was fighting with a dangerous animal and it claw me." said Sam. "Now that's a little better." said Sheila. As she whisper again into her dad's ear.

"What a Owl?" ask the doctor. Because it got you good and you came to the right place for a technical shot." said the doctor. "I would like to do some blood work on you. And the doctor ask Sam to do a urine sample. But Sam stood up immediately and got lightheaded again for what ever reason.

The doctor immediately admitted him Because Sam looks alright but not alright. "Mr. Bentford I believe that you sir are a diabetic I put money on it." said the doctor. "What! I don't believe you doc!" said Sam. "Listen Mr. Bentford I can tell certain symptoms with signs of bad health sir." said the doctor. "I being in this line of work for almost thirty two years and I know a diabetic when I see one." said the doctor. "I still need that urine specimen from you sir." said the doctor. When Sam went into the men's room to drop urine.

Sheila kinda open up to the physician by telling every detail about her father's health.

Now Sam has been in the men's room for five minutes or more as the doctor and Sheila looks at each other thinking that Sam shouldn't take that long for a drop of urine. "Dad! Are you ok in there?"ask Sheila."Yes I'am cool." said Sam.

Seconds later Sam comes out with the small container half filled with urine. "I just had a small problem I couldn't pee for a minute and when I did it kinda hurts when I do." said Sam. "Now it seens to me that your prostate has enlarge on you sir and how long have you experience this situation sir?" ask the doctor. "I can't remember when but when I do go it seens like I can't use it at times." said Sam. "What i'am going to do is prescribe you some medication to take before bedtime and what that is going to do is make it easier for you to urinate and some for your diabetes also." said the doctor. "Well alright." said Sam. "I hate getting old." said Sam. "All this comes with age Mr. Bentford sir." said the doctor. "We are going to keep you for a day to run a few test on you." "Would that be ok?" ask the doctor. "I didn't have any intention to come here and stay." said Sam. "Dad stay and let them do what needs to be done. Ok?" ask Sheila. "Jonny and I will be ok." said Sheila. Sam had a look that can kill right about now. Sam doesn't like doctor's and hospital's because they tell you stuff that you don't want to hear but must know if it's a matter of life or death. "I be back tomorrow to get you dad." said Sheila. "I really don't like this at all. Staying in this (explicit) hospital." said sam. "Hey! your gonna be fine and quit being on the offensive side of things." said Sheila."Sorry sweetie. Thank you for coming here with me." said Sam. "Your my dad and I love you." said Sheila. "And I love you the same." said Sam.

As Sheila departs from her father's side she kisses him on his forehead and tells him that she love him and then she left. The minute Sheila left. Sam fell asleep with a nurse trying to draw blood out of Sam left arm. "What in the hell are you doing!?" ask Sam. "Mr. Bentford I need to draw some blood from you sir." said the nurse. "Pardon me sorry ma'am." said Sam. "It's ok I know that your trying to rest sir." said the nurse. "I hate hospital's I hate doctor's too but I love the nurse's." said Sam. "Oh ain't you so sweet." said the nurse. "What happen to your arm?" ask the nurse.

"If I told you You wouldn't believe me." said Sam. "Well try me." said the nurse. "I was fighting something evil it's something I never thought in my entire life going up against but me and my kids are still alive." said Sam. "What did you go up against? A owl?" ask the nurse. "I rather not say anymore." said Sam.

Therefore sam knows in his heart that people would think of crazy when looking and talking with him while he is trying to discussed the situation. But the right patients and enough timing would reveal the truth. As Sam put it before that no one would believe him or his kids and that's why Sam need his children not to mention the situation to others. While sounding like a illusional nut job Sam intent to start the conversation then cut it off dry. Because he knows no one would take him seriously about him and his children fighting a mysterious creature.

Because to some it would sound like more of a dream then reality or to see it to believe it. Ain't it funny how Sam and children how everything seems to fall right into their laps?

Trying to grasp the truth behind everything. In the meantime Jon is talking with one of his friends that holds a position over at the university doing their best into determining the so call dna that wasted from the creature what's in it.

Was a chemical plasma of weird hormones and animal testosterones. "So Jon where did you get this from?" ask Greg Jaymes. "Man I founded in my backyard then I scrape some of it up and put it in this jar." said Jon. "Hey we may be living among a new species never know." said Greg Jaymes.

"But I think you may have something here." said Greg Jaymes. "I like to do quite a bit of testing on this and I will give you a shout in a couple of days." Cool?" ask Greg. "Ok I be looking for your call so long Greg." said

Jon. Now Jon is headed back to the house. But he is going to the tracks to look at something near the house. As he parks the truck into the driveway he walks to the backyard on over to the corn field on to the tracks Jon looks both ways and no trains insight but there was a dwarf signal that was lit red for trains to come to a complete stop. As Jon was standing on the track bed he looks over on the other set of tracks there was a pile of dry dead flesh lying near the second set of tracks.

But Jon took off running back to the barn to look for a box or a container to put what he has found near the tracks into for to secure it for Greg to look at. Then it hit Jon that he would need some gloves to contained it. Not far off from where Jon has seen those pieces of flesh the creature is watching his every move. By the time Jon went to the barn and back to the tracks to recover what he has found A red on gray locomotive was coming on fast with the loud sound of it's horn and the engineer stop to see what is Jon doing near the tracks. And was warned to stay away from the track-bed and told that he was also trepassing. "Sorry sir It want happen it again." said Jon. Jon grab every bit of what he has discover is in a box and as Jon walk back towards the barn thinking smiling about how much money he would get off if he would sell to the university. As he would put away his small discovery into the barn then go into the house and notify Greg Jaymes to bring him another piece of evidence of what the creature has left behind needs to be examined.

Now that Sheila has returned from the doctor office without Sam presence. Jon told Sheila to come out to the barn with him to show her something that he has found at the tracks and the story is getting much weirder as it go on about the creature. "Look what I found over at the tracks." said Jon.

"Oh wow what is that!?" ask Sheila. "It's dry dead flesh from a human torso or something." said Jon. "Now! What are you going to do with that?" ask Sheila. "Before you walk into the house I was getting ready to call Greg over at the university to let him know that I have another piece of evidence for him to examined." said Jon. "That is sickining if you ask me." said Sheila. "Oh yeah Sheila! Where is our father?" ask Jon.

"The doctor admitted him into the hospital's to stay for some testing." said Sheila. "Our father's health is getting so bad so! we both need to keep an eye on him." said Sheila.

"Oh you know what he tried to do in the doctor's office?" ask Sheila. "What?" ask Jon. "He was up there lying to the doctor about his arm telling him that he damage his arm in the barn." said Sheila. Jon (laughing). "Well that's dad."said Jon. As the sun begins to set. The air starts to change from cool to cold. And both Jon and Sheila heads into the house for the evening without their father's presence. But Jon knows what Sam has taught him when he isn't home. That he's the man of the house. And no exception. On Jon's mind is when does this evil creature is willing to strikes unexpectedly tonight tomorrow or the day afterwards? It's where the point of putting the guards down or leaving them up. Just don't know when. It's typical to have a accident but to worried about getting mull by a monster wasn't a reality: it was a dream or a nightmare. Now it's a reality for the Bentford's and the town of Lajunta.

Saw and Not See

Chpt X

As Sam lying in the hospital's bed thinking of his children's well being he nods off into a deep sleep into a nightmare of watching his whole family being destroyed by this terrible and mindless creature. While trying to save them from the grips of evil Sam was last to be taken from life's itself.

But as Sam tossed and turned until he worked the (iv) intravenous that's in his arm out of place. While shouting out loud "Leave my family alone take me!" shouts Sam.

"Huh What what!?" said Sam. When the nurse had touch him to see if Sam was ok "Just having a silly nightmare so sorry for shouting out like that." said Sam. "I truly understand sir can I get you anything sir?" ask the nurse.

"Yes a cold beer please." said Sam. "Well sir I can't make that happen but I will definitely get you a cold beverage with some ice. Now how about that?" ask the nurse. "I was just pulling your leg."said Sam."But that will be fine." said Sam. "One cold beverage with ice coming up." said the nurse. In Sam's head was how much did that nurse hear him say? Now Sam would have to find out with a question of two by asking her what was said. Even though Sam was trying to hit on the same nurse for a minute. As Sam thought again the nurse is beautiful to look upon she is great in stature built with a nice set of digital display for a man like Sam to go crazy for. But Sam definitely has to get June out of his head before moving on with his life.

Because his children's would love to see him happy and not constantly alone. As the nurse comes in with a can cola with ice "Hey beautiful when I was having a nightmare in by any chance did you hear what I was saying?" ask Sam.

The nurse started laughing and sat down next to Sam's bed and she said "not really Mr. Bentford all I heard you say was leave my family alone and take me." said the nurse.

"I said that?" ask Sam."Yes sir."said the nurse. As the she started laughing again then she looks at Sam and ask him, "Who do you want to take you? The boogie man." said the nurse. Sam had to laugh at that in which Sam needed a good laugh he needed some humorus to take his mind off of the bad that enter into his life for whatsoever reason is still lingering from day to day. "By the way what is your name?

If you don't mind." ask Sam. "Well since you must know i'am Terra McKenzie." said the nurse. "Well Terra i'am glad to meet you dear." said Sam. "you are leaving tomorrow right?" ask the nurse. "I think I might wanna stay another day if possible." said Sam. "That would be upon the doctor to look at." said the nurse. "By the way you said you didn't like hospital's doctor's etc so why the change of heart?" ask the nurse. "Must you really know?" ask Sam.

"Yes Mr. Bentford I like to know and you are going to tell me right?" ask the nurse. "It's you that make me wanna stay you reminds me of my wife who passed away of thirty something years and that's why i'am tickle to death when I saw you." said Sam. "Oh Mr. Bentford." "Terra call me Sam please."said Sam."Ok Sam i'am very flatter of your words until I don't know what to do." said the nurse as she giggle to herself. "When I get outta here can I take you to dinner or a movie?" ask Sam. "You know what yes you can I would like that." said the nurse. "Great it's a date." said Sam.

Now Sam has developed a friendship with a nurse who is thirty years younger his youth. Actually Terra and Sheila could be sisters both around the same age group and very territoral and very protected of the one they love. And most of all they both are women. So Sam can see a lot of jealousy moodiness enviness and wants plenty attention. But Sheila's eyes saw her first love when she was born and that is her father so Sheila has every right to act the way she would about her father if another woman shows up on the door step. Terra on the other hand is a mindful person that is well groom for motherhood and a wife to be. She speaks when spoken to. She can be a bit controlling cause the field of work she does. Jon was a momma's boy why Sheila was daddy little angel. Both Jon and Sheila alike are very protected of their father's well being. With one parent gone they are very grateful to have their father with them. And misses momma June dearly. But it will be a huge surprises when Terra starts coming over for supper and staying the night with Sam. And Sheila of all people isn't going to like that at all. Jonny may get a little upset with his father for having this younger lady to play a part into their lives. May be unfair to both Jon and Sheila cause June's has being gone for ten months close to a year. And a younger version of June trying to play motherhood to children her age.

Meanwhile back at the Bentford's residences Jon and Sheila are busy around the house trying to clean and make things look organize and neat. Jon is cleaning his room and livingroom while Sheila is preparing dinner and washing laundry.

Then the phone rings as Sheila walks over to answer it. With sam on the other end lettting Sheila know he is ready to come on home tomorrow afternoon "i have a surprise for you and your brother."said Sam."Tell me now please dad." said Sheila. "No it's a surprise if I told you now then there isn't a surprise."said Sam."Ok I wait until tomorrow." said Sheila."Where is your brother?"ask Sam."He's in his room cleaning." said Sheila. "Has that thing being back there?" ask Sam. "No dad." said Sheila. "Great I see you here by eleven thirty sweetie." said Sam. "Ok dad eleven thirty it is."said Sheila.

Jon just came out of his room to check on his sister's well being and of course then look on the outside of the house.

Because they are there alone and not to take any chances of letting their guards down for nothing. "Who was that you talking to?" ask Jon. "Daddy." said Sheila. "Is he alright?" ask Jon. "He was letting me know when to pick him up from the hospital tomorrow."said Sheila. "Also he said he has a surprise for the both of us." said Sheila. "O' Boyee, I wander if he is going to stop drinking."said Jon. "Hey how much longer until dinner?"ask Jon. "Ten minutes the most." said Sheila.

As going back to his bedroom Jon stops in the middle of the hallway listening to a humming noise of a engine coming pass the house. But Jon went to grab his twelve gage from the livingroom coffee table headed to the back door to see what will take place. With Sheila in back of him with a butcher knife in hand ready to go to war with this wothless monster.

Well the train kept on going east it didn't have any intention to stop which was a good thing: cause both Jon and Sheila wasn't in no shape to fight a creature that size it would take at least three people to handle that monster.As the Bentford's starts to look like fighting a huge cancer with paws and talons that keep on coming back and sit's in remission. But the right time is going to come sooner or later. The truth all about how this creature came to do what it's doing.

"That was close I thought we both had to fight this thang again without dad not being here." said Jon. "I will be sleeping on the sofa tonight. Just in case this evil demon decides to show up."said Jon. "I can sleep in the recliner if necessary." said Sheila. "No you can sleep in your own bed sis if you hear any noise out here then you come a running and swinging ok?" ask jon. "Ok." said Sheila. Still not to know that the predator is ways from carrying out another attack on the Bentford's offsprings by late nite it will come creeping around again for to eliminating the whole family if can. But one thing only this mindless creature doesn't think about the danger it put itself into it has being wounded twice by the same family but by wounding it can tell the truth later on.

The night went quite well without Sam presence and no invasion whatsoever from the creature with Jon trying to get a hold of Greg Jaymes over at the university but Greg is not answering his phone for whatsoever reason not to. So Jon walks out to the barn to get that dry dead flesh he found at the tracks and man! The barn had a terrible odour inside til no one can go in. So Jon opens both sides of the barn to air it out. But one thing has gone wrong and that is that the barn mices and the rats has gotten hold of that discovery of Jon's and eaten it. Jon had a disappointed look for not taking inconsideration of the barns rodent problem before putting it in there.

Now that the evidents is no longer around thanks to the rodents Jon took it upon himself to seek more evidents to get this creature's crimes. So he walks back to the tracks together up more then before. As coming to the first set of tracks Jon realize that there was a on coming engine that looks like the creature's engine. And Jon turned to go back to the cornfield to hide but it wasn't nothing there to hide from so Jon stood there boldly but scared as ever. But that day Jon stood up like a man is suppose to. See Jon thought in his mind that this creature has taken somebody precious from him and his family that one somebody is his mother.

So to Jon the creature deserve to die. If needed to fight all night so be it. Jon puts it eye for an eye tooth for an tooth without a weapon involved the looks of this fight wouldn't take long. Because something that is seven foot tall with paws and talons would be over in a instant. But Jon and a weapon in hand can defeat this evil and wicked creature with a couple of slugs to it's dome. Without hesitation one load and click and bang! It's over with.

Now it seem like it harder for to catch this thang on the spot but it's come up unexpected to kill with it's horror looks to terrorize which it makes everthing gruesome. And as the engine passes by pulling another locomotive with boxcars behind it Jon was a bit of relieve when he saw a engineer with common courtesy wave at him. Because he saw the locomotive and not see the colors of the red on black with the letters "let's go to hell". It can be hard to see it face to front then the easy way of seeing the lettering from the sides of the engine. "Jonny!! calls Sheila i'am going to pick up dad we will be back shortly." said Sheila. "Ok!" said Jon. As jon continues to dig for more evidents to find against the creature. As Jon dig further the creature sees Jon's whereabouts right about now to come and strike and fight for a meal and probably win but with Jon it will be a fight to the finished. While the creature is zooming in on Jon out in the opening and away from the nest is what the creature love about it For his prey to make it so easy to get to. With it's eagle veiw sight it can zoom in on it prey very well. But you can smell it coming but can't see it because it has the capabilties of making itself invisible.

As the creature stays up in the trees it decides not to attack Jon for some reason maybe it's not after Jon it's wants someone else that's in the famliy. After all Jon was the one to wounded it the first time then Sam did it the second time.

But the creature only attacks when both men are at hand so it wants both men to wipe out both generations if can. As long as weapons are at both men's disposal the creature doesn't have a clue nor chance into destroying a bloodlinage.

As Jon starts to wrap up his investigate. He walks back to the house and wait on his father and sister to get back from the hospital's to see how his dad is doing and to see what is the surprise is all about. What a surprise visit from someone just sitting in the driveway so Jon opens the door to see who is it in the driveway. What do you know? It's Ed out of all of Lajunta he just sitting in his car gazing at the house. "Mr. Dart! Is that you?" ask Jon. "Yes Jon it's me." said Ed. "Are you going to come in?"ask Jon."I would but I wounded my leg pretty bad just tell your dad I was here." said Ed. "I let him know that you stop to see him." said Jon. As Ed rolls up his window and then take off headed to his house he was cussing up a storm cause Sam wasn't at home but was mad because he was in pain so much pain until he wants to kill. As he went up the road to cross the tracks he was looking to see where to park his car for a moment to fight with his pain. But being shot while transform into something else the pain isn't as great when you are a monster. Its hurts bad when only in human form.

With Ed's leg damage from a gun shot wound it's hard to come around those that you pretend to love or trying to destroyed. Because of a long awakening hatred that cause your heart to become a evil reckoning and not know it. But having a conditonal love for someone or something can be a beacon of light. Now Ed and Sam are bestfriend's all throughout their school years but Sam was the ladies man that always get the women And Ed wasn't cute enough to have what Sam had to pull any woman his way. So Ed became a little jealous of his bestfriend until they stop talking to each other for almost fifteen years or more. So the hate has grew over the years.But Ed never told Sam that he works for the railroad company or engineer a locomotive he never told Sam anything about his life after school days.

So the real hatred comes when Ed and June were good friends until Sam shows up on the scene til June falls in love with Sam and put Ed on the back burner actually pushed old Ed to the curb. And June's allegiance to Sam was made.

And that angers Ed entirely causing his heart to grew even evil until he has givin up on the way of being good. Evil was the way to make thing real and possible. Sitting up one night real late til Ed started talking to himself then he ask for satan to come into his life completely for guidiance and unlimited powers to do his work alone. Then Ed told the devil that he needed a covenent to bear the consequences by giving the devil his soul for the powers to do so much evil to those that is a good and wholesome person.

Ed went to bed that night believeing everything that he ask for that he shall get it. Without a shadow of doubt Ed wake up the next day with many capabilties and now he is very invincible can't overcome him neither out do him. Now Ed's leg is wrapped good in gauze until he has to unwrap it to clean it every now and then to let it breath. To Ed he will change the gauze when he get to his place as coming from the opposite direction Sheila and Sam passes by Ed's car that was sitting on the side of the tracks. "Dad wasn't that Ed's car on the side of the railroad tracks?" ask Sheila. "I did see a car but couldn't tell if it was him." said Sam. "Maybe it was him and again maybe not."said Sam.

"My question is why is his car sitting near the railroad tracks?" ask Sheila. "You know Ed is a bit of a estrange one who is a good friend but also a enemy at times too." said sam. "I thought that is really odd for him to sit that close to the tracks for a locomotive to come and smack his but to death." said Sheila. "Well we my sweet daughter aren't going to worried about Edward Dart." said Sam. As getting close to home Sam started to let Sheila in on the small surprise that he was going to share with both Jon and Sheila. But it wouldn't be fair to share with the one and not the other. So Sam thought it would be best to tell them both at the same time and get it over with. Because he knows his children can act a little funny towards others if they don't know you quite well. Jon would gaze at anyone he doesn't know and was told that it is impolite to gaze at someone for a long period of time. And Sheila want talk to you unless she is spoken too and Sheila will keep it short and simple and cut and dry. With a little bit of rolling her eyes if not approve.

So bring a guest to the dinner table can be very intriguing, if not knowning that person all so well. So that person will remained a mystery for a while. Until the right time for everyone to be comfortable with each other. So Sam go into the house to gather both Jon and Sheila and explain the great news of meeting a nurse at the hospital. "Her name is Terra McKenzie and I ask her out on a date and she said that she would like that." said Sam. As Jon and Sheila just looks at one another with silence. Then Jon told his dad that "He is proud of him for meeting someone new that can keep him happy but if she can't then she is going to have problems from Sheila and I."said Jon.Now Sheila is asking questions like she is Sam's mother asking the son before his first date what to do what not to do. "How old is this lady if you don't mind telling us?" ask Sheila. "I think that you and her are around the same age or older."said Sam. "Dad!! you know better! To date a kid!." said Sheila. "How could you live with yourself!?" ask Sheila. "Wait a minute Sheila it's nothing wrong with dad date a younger woman besides she can keep him occupied and healthy so again it's nothin wrong with that." said Jon. "Dad what in the heck do you want with a girl my age?" ask Sheila. "The truth is she reminds me of your mother in the face with a warm smile and soft spoken voice and everything that your mother did she does also it's like history is repeating itself." said Sam.

"So kids I don't want to upset you both I just needs a com panion to eat with and to stay on me about my health ok?" ask Sam. As both Jon and Sheila reply "ok". "She better not (explicit) up cause when she does I will be the one all over her butt." said Sheila. "Sweetie you don't have to worried about that." ok?" ask Sam. As Sheila rolled her eyes and walks away in anger. Just like a woman to do when she isn't getting whatsoever she deserve. As a man would understands another man's point on having a younger woman in his life.

Now sam would tried to hold things together between both daughter and courtship of Terra McKenzie will be very chanllenging. But Sam also understands if his kids don't approve of Terra McKenzie just as yet. Because June has being missing for a year and Sam and both kids misses her dearly.

And there isn't any denial from both husband and kids that Mrs. June was indeed a great wife and mother to both Sam and kid's.

Nightmares of the Innocent

Chpt XI

As sam walks into the kitchen the kitchen was very clean and very organize like if June was there. Actually the whole house was absolutly clean and neat. "Wow! Thanx to the both of you for cleaning up. It seen to me that I just let this place go and not know that people do come by to see me." said sam. "I really thank God for you two." said Sam. "We both are very gracious to have a father like you too." said Jon. While Sheila was in her bedroom there with a attitude and lots of pouting.

To her alone she's daddy number one girl for other women to get pass her wasn't an option. It's more less a borderline fence with a female rottweiler that is devoted and courages -ous. Sheila is ever bit of her mother June when it comes to other women June has taken pre caution because she knew how women are wired for confusion and sometimes unstableness. So Sheila do have some of her mother's traits of operating in general for everyday life.

Now with thanksgiving is next week the family hasn't contacted no one neither June's side of the family Sam's side of the family and friends of course. With June's disappearance the family hasn't being reaching out to others like they often to do. So staying among themselves is the plan for right now unless someone calls on getting together. "Sheila! Can you ride with us to the store we are going to look for a ham and turkey for next week dinner?" ask Sam. "If you both don't mind I rather stay here and finish cleaning the other parts of the house." said Sheila. "Wait honey you aren't coming? And why not?" ask Sam. "Look! I just don't feel like going nowhere!" said Sheila. As Sheila yells at her dad with a lot of anger and it's unusual coming from her. As she runs to here room and slams the door behind here. Then sam just stood there look hurt from what just had happen coming from his baby girl. Then turns to Jon and said "I didn't mean to hurt anyone and especially my baby girl." said Sam. "Well dad you isn't going to please everybody and Sheila is going to be Sheila matter what." said Jon.

Besides she will eventually get over it."said Jon. The fact is that another woman is coming on board and sheila can't deal with it. Having another woman besides her mother in the same household as her. Sheila doesn't have any tolerance for another woman that's not her mother. Now Sam thinks it's a bad ideal to meet someone else and not ask his childrens for their approval first. But it isn't going to change a thing between him andTerra McKenzie meeting one another it's going to happen sooner or later."Jon my dear son you are right she will eventually get over it I have to let her cry sometime instead of pampering her Sheila is a grown woman." said Sam.

Now Sheila is plotting to leave the house for good and once and for all. Because in her heart she thinks what her dad has done it's devastating to her heart and causing her mind to do other wise. Now she's really misses Jay's presence very much indeed. When things weren't right at home Sheila often run's to Jay for comfort and confined into him for refuge.

But the next few days will play out to see how things would go. So Sam has his hands full with a slight rebellious daugther and a creature to worried about. With the weekend approaching quickly and Sam is going to meet Terra this weekend coming to go to see a movie first then supper afterwards then a walk downtown then home.

It would be great for a man like Sam to get out for all that the man has being through it would be good for him to be with someone that can take his mind off of the worse things in his life. For serveral people has called on Sam to look at there automobile's but all Sam can do is think about the days ahead and even practice his manners as opening the doors for a lady. Just like the good ol' days when June was around but a different generation and times.

As Jon was talking to his father about the dry dead flesh that he has found near the railroad tracks and what had happens afterwards. Sam's head was in the clouds blotting out anything and everything around him. But Jon notices his father's mind is all on this lady with his nose wide open it's ashamed to see him sad but also it's great to see him in a fined mood. So Jon went to the kitchen to tried to get in touch with Greg Jaymes over at the university: but still no success so Jon will keep trying his best to get in touch with him. For more on the DNA that he had looked at. As he would know Greg Jaymes is calling him back with some of good news with also some bad news that is going to rock Jon's world."Hello!" said Jon. "Hey Jon Greg here I started to call you lastnight but I got so busy with the wife and kids so forgive me for not calling you back sooner." said Greg Jaymes. "It's ok so what did you find out about that dna?" ask Jon. "The good news is the university would like to do a further study on this. And the bad news is no funding to uphold for further reseach." said Greg Jaymes"Hey Jon!

You don't mind telling me where did you get this from?" ask Greg Jaymes. "Well Greg since no funding I can't tell you that sir." said Jon. "Ok! I deserve that." wow!" said Greg. "So you not going to tell me?" ask Greg. "Nope." said Jon. "So what is it going to take for you to tell me what I need to know about this dna?" ask Greg.

"What are you prepared to give me for the info in return?" ask jon. As both Jon and Greg going to and fro on the small issues like if it was a barter services. "Hey Greg! What did you find out about that dna?" ask Jon. "Well here it is I see a mixed between a animal and man's dna which is not common at all." said Greg. "But very rare in this day and age so how did you find and where did you recover this?" ask Greg Jaymes. "Hear we go again Greg! I can't tell you that for one if I told you c'mon man! You wouldn't believe me if I told you at all." said Jon. "Why don't you try me my friend and see." said Greg Jaymes. "I tell you what let's get together for a coffee or beverage and talk this out ok?" ask Greg.

"I have a better ideal let's talk over a beer and burger& fries at T&R beer house on the corner of Eugenio and Bess rd so what do you say?" ask Jon. "Hey man! that's not a bad ideal i'am down with that."said Greg Jaymes."How about the weekend this weekend coming?" ask jon. "Ok great." said Greg Jaymes."Well I see you there." said Jon.

Now the day and place was set for the two can come and put a piece of evidence in perpective. But a bad bad ideal over a beer. Because Jon is like his father when just one and a half pitcher of beer makes it also tipsy then comes the talking outside of the neck. And say whatsoever comes to mind. And tell all and everything there is. While intoxicated. So a bad ideal for jon's behalf.

After a long and tired evening jon was sitting at the kitchen table thinking in running a trap in the middle of the cornfield deep enough to hold it down to kill it. Then sam comes in humming a tune from the pass while Jon just gaze at his father's unperculiar weirdness that wasn't there months ago and now it's like he is a new man with a million dollars smile and walk. "Hey son. What's up?" ask Sam. "You is what's up dad." said Jon.

"You acting like Sheila and I isn't here anymore and this young woman! Got you on a damn string dad." said Jon. "Now you starts to sound like your sister now." said Sam. "Well dad maybe Sheila is right about you dating a younger woman it don't fit." said Jon. As Jon leaves the kitchen with a slight attitude with his dad's happiness. As Sam slowly sit into one of the chairs around the kitchen table thinking again maybe his children are trying to tell him something that he is missing. Maybe his children are right about everything. Minutes late jon approach his dad at the kitchen table. "I have a question for you. Do you still care about mom? Do you still love us?" ask Jon.

"Jonny sit son I will always love you and your sister you both are my seeds from my own loins so how can I stop love you both? And yes! I misses your mom a lot I still love her also the crazy thing about that is she still love us the same." said Sam. "I'am just tired of being without a companion that can help me to be a good man that i'am now." said Sam.

"I say once that the both of you and Sheila meets Terra maybe you both would like her. Then that like would turn into loving her like lovin me."said Sam. "Dad all we can do is take things one day at a time right?"ask Jon."Yes son your are right." said Sam. As both Sam and Jon sat at the kitchen table having a father to son chat here comes Sheila for a cold drink from the fridge as she ignored both men headed back to her peaceful bedroom but Sam ask if he could talk to her for a moment. Now Jon departs to go to another part of the house as Sheila sat to hear her father out. "Hey honey I was just telling your brother that I will always love you both you both are mines until the good Lord calls me home in heaven "said Sam. "Dad! Don't start talking about dying to me please!" said Sheila. "No sweetie i'am talking about how much I love you and Jon with all my heart and how much I misses your mother." said Sam. But dad! What about this other young girl that's going to play mom to me and Jon!?"ask Sheila. "Sheila! Listen to me there isn't a woman enough that can take your mother's place in our hearts sweetheart so you need to get that outta of your beautful head." said Sam. "I told Jon that I need a companion that I can do things with and help keep me healthy at the same time." said Sam. "Do things like what?" ask Sheila."Well like going to dinner a walk in the park and a good movie to go see together stuff like that." said Sam.

"But dad tell me the truth your not! Thinking about marrying this young girl are you?" ask Sheila. "I'am definitely not sure at what happens afterwards."said Sam"Honey please believe me when I don't know how this courtship will play out." said Sam. "Like I said before let her butt messes up then she's mines." said Sheila. "Dad i'm not playing about this (explicit)."said Sheila. As getting up from the kitchen table Sheila walks over to give her father a kiss on his right cheek and then telling him the words he loves to hear from both jon and Sheila. "Goodnight dad I love you." said Sheila.

As everyone's is set to going to bed except Sam of course is about to call Terra before it gets any later. As Sam gets a bit comfortable while dialing Terra's number. Until he heard a thump on the back porch then Sam hangs up the phone and went to get his winchester and get Jon while at it. And rush to the back door to look out to see what's going on.

"Jonny! Come here for a moment I believe this thang has shown up again out on the back porch to terrorize us once more." said Sam. "For all week long this creature hasn't being here at all and now you are home and it decide to come calling on us for destruction." said Jon. As both men looking out the back door and of the window to see if they can spot it. They looked out and yes it was just standing there and gazing grawling with a sorted of spear like javalin in it paws. Like if it wanted one or both men to come out and oppose it instead it came up to the back door and with a strong thrust with the javalin going through the door striking both jon and sam in the abdominal area. Killing both men at the same time as it spoke the words "Now let's go to hell."

The words are on the side of it's engine. As dragging both men back to it engine with Sam and jon screaming for help but the life has gone out of both men. And by the time they reaches the locomotive Sam wake up in a cold sweat at the kitchen table where he fail of sleep with a nasty little nightmare. As Sam walks to check on jon first he was also knockout and then he left to check on Sheila and she was fast to sleep. Then Sam climb into his own bed trying to go to back to sleep but after that nightmare to Sam it was a little disturbing to him so he just lying in bed thinking about all the good he had throughout his life and now here comes the bad to out weigh the good.

So instead of going back to sleep Sam got up and went to the livingroom and sat in front of the fireplace to iron out somethings in his life with the house as quiet as it is there Sam can really think while sitting in front of a cozy fire. So with the fire as warm as it is Sam decides to have a cup of coffee instead of a beer then Sam notice that he is changing his life slowly and not knowning it at all. It's about four thirty in the morning when Sam glances at the clock. In Sam's mind he wasn't sure if he talk with Terra last night or not so he's not quite sure what was said in the conversation.

But was still wandering about that nightmare he had which was a hint that the fight of survival still continues on. For as his family goes he knows he will protect them with all means necessary. From far off there was a train coming from the east of town pulling automobile's and military equipement moving with all that ton's of weight Sam heard it and went to get his piece just in case if the creature may want to start war again this morning early. What a coincidence that Jon heard the same and gotten up with his shotgun in hand coming from his bedroom lock and loaded.

Now with both Sam and Jon standing at the back door looking out watching and waiting for somethin to jump and get smoke. It's crazy it's funny to every sound of a engine that the father and son would need their weapons for protection.

But for better results in staying alive it's a survival game to the finish. As the train is about out of sight both son and the father can be at ease from a self made drill in order to stay alive while their lives marches to a new drum line.

But not liking the sounds of death gazing in from the other side. Now the day has arrived for Sam's date with Terra mckenzie and Jon's day to find out more on the creature's dna.

So that leaves Sheila all alone to herself. But Sam is suggesting that Sheila could be a chaperone for him and watch his behavior towards Terra by being a naughty old man. But Sheila is being very differcult at this time and not trying to meet another female that isn't allowed to be in her world.

But sam hasn't ask Sheila yet by knowning her reaction would be already or just assuming what Sheila wouldn't do.

With all that is going on Sam doesn't want to jeopardize his daugthher's life that if left alone by herself in the house.

For a sinister dangerous and ugly creature to lay paws on so Jon would ask his sister to hangout with him instead of Sam on his young new date. Now who would wants to hangout with a father on a date with someone that's the same age as the youngest child?. That's what Jon has thought of in his mind. As Jon getting up to make way to his sister's bedroom to see if she would be interested in riding with him for fun.

As Sheila answered her room door "Yeah!" said Sheila.

"What are you doing today?" ask Jon. "Nothing! Why?" ask Sheila. "Can you go with me over to the university i'am going over to check on something." said Jon. "Heck yeah!

I will go with you when are you going?" ask Sheila. "Well it's friday so about noon!" said Jon. "Ok."said Sheila. As soon as Jon insisted that Sheila to come alone with him Jon went to let his father know so he doesn't have to worried a bit about Sheila's well being. As everyone's starts to get the day going. Sam sat around thinking about his nightmare encounter without saying anything to Jon which was smart on sam behalf because Jon would sit around and wait or take action. See Sam's date isn't until a little later so he makes some calls to the people who needs their automobiles look at for service. But the people he reaches out to aren't answering their phones because of the holiday is upon them.

So Jon and Sheila is getting ready to leave the house. But Jon knows that leaving his father in the house alone isn't a good ideal to do with this creature on the prowl. And sheila thought so as well so both Jon and Sheila tried to wait another hour before leaving. But Jon also knows that it's wrong to have Greg to wait for another hour so Jon isn't sure what to do.Lucky is Jon Greg calls to see if their meeting is still on for the evening. "Hey Greg" said Jon."Hey Jon are we still going to meet this evening?" ask Greg. "I was definitely planning on it." said Jon. "I will see you there later." said Greg. As both Jon and Sheila make their way out the door Sam asking his children where are they going and how long are they going to be? "Dad the thing is you need to go and have a good time." said Jon. As Sheila stood there shaking her head while walking out of the door.

"Be careful you two." said Sam. "We be back as soon as possible." said Jon. Then the door shut. As leaving the driveway here comes Edward Dart pulling into the driveway honking his horn for Sam to come out on the porch. But as ed sat in his car with a still wounded leg he knows that sam would ask questions about his leg if he had gotten out of the car. So his best bet is to stay put. Because it would look so obvious with a wounded leg. And the question is how is so for ed to have gotten wounded like he has? Sam did shoot that night a pretty good shot. But sam doesn't know anymore about his so call bestfriend and that's what going to hurt sam the most.

Like all these years ed was suppose to be sam and june's friend but all he was trying to get was revenge on the couple and their family. From years of frustration built up inside and hatred for Sam for taking June's friendship is coming for to wipeout the whole Bentford family with a swifty kill. "Hey Ed hows it going?" ask Sam from his porch. "Great! I thought I should stop and see hows things with the family." said Ed from his car. "Oh things are getting better for us everyday around here." said Sam. "So are they huh?" ask Ed with a sort of a wicked grin. "Hey Ed! I don't mean to be rude but I have a date to attend to here shortly so I talk to you later on sometime ok?" ask Sam. "Well I don't mean to hold you up!" said Ed. As Sam watching Ed take off pulling out of his driveway Sam notice Ed's bumper on his car was cover with smear blood stains. But Sam walks into his house thinking that color of blood stains he has seen before See Sam has forgotten about the night that him and Jon was fighting the creature in the front yard under the tree.

And where he pump one into the leg of the creature.

And as Ed leaves the Bentford's home he was using explicit words like it ain't no ones business mad as heck. Because the creature in him seems not getting the job done Ed wants Samuel Bentford dead. Just as the wife was taken Sam can be next of course the children has to be dealt with also. As Ed driving and thinking to himself "how can a man like Sam Bentford can look me in the eye's and say that he is my bestfriend?" as Ed thought. By determining the death of your nemesis in human form was how so. And then place an attack on them in a creature stake of mind.

So in human form the mind knows right from wrong but in a creature's stake there isn't no conscience at all to do what's right. So Ed has taken innocent lives and destroyed families emotions bitterly. Because of his long hatred for a man and his family To Ed there isn't no talking it out over a beer not even at a football game the creature is the way to solve the problems that Ed has by killing. To Ed he has notice it's so hard to kill off something that is good. And evil is trying to prevailed but can't. So that's why Ed is so angry and upset because things aren't going according to his plans. But to Ed it's time for a transfiguration and go get his locomotive for to offset lives and count for casualties from evil deeds.

Sam is about to leave to meet his date for the hour but before leaving Sam had another glance at his nightmare for some reason but didn't stick around to go through the whole scenerio Sam was so anxious to get to his young date until he forgot to lock the front door and left his keys on the kitchen table then he realized he wouldn't got far from where he stood. As far over the way Ed was looking on his so call bestfriend and watching his every move until Ed decides to follow Sam and his young date around town. But Sam wasn't aware of the situation. If so Sam would probably stopped speaking to him anymore for the reason of spying on him like that.

As sam walks up to meet Terra he gives her a meet and greet kiss on her right cheek then he takes her by her soft right hand and they both walks towards the resturant doors."Hey Terra you look amazing this evening." said sam. "And you look so handsome yourself." said Terra. "Why thank you." said Sam. "Shall we go in and get us a table before it get to crowded?" ask Sam. "Why certainly." said Terra. As Ed is watching from a distant sitting in his car mad as heck breathing and cussing like a sailor would do when his duty is required more then what he has done already. "Wow she is young and beautiful but what is she doing with him?

Creep." as Ed thinking out loud to himself. As Ed can see Terra and Sam through the glass window of the restaurant holding hands standing there conversating with one another wandering what in the heck are they talking about. But Ed wants to go in and interuppted their meal but can't with a bad leg that was shot by sam himself. So Ed just sit in his vehicle there in so much agony and pain. Groaning and cussing as the creature starts to come out with his eyes turning red from blue and his fingers would grow long and then talons would come next. As Ed starts to transfigurate right there in his car it would be a bad and ugly scene. Because he couldn't hold his anger for another day. Instead he was trying to exposed himself then and there. Ed was going to scared half of the towns civilians that was in the country style restaurant. The scene of Sam and Terra was really getting to Ed so he left the romantic scene with hurt and hate on his agenda. So leaving he skidded out of the parking lot of the restaurant on his way to his place and then off to his engine so he can take it out on other people that crosses the tracks of decietful. But before going home he slowed down to take a look at Sam's home which no one wasn't home Ed was so mad til he grab a small rock and thru it at the front window breaking the glass pane for whatever reason he is just that evil to do so.

Then Ed returned to get into his vehicle then he left grining to himself calling sam names which some was worse then others. But his hatred for Sam has grown over a year span after killing June the conspiring comes to killing all of the Bentford's slow quick and horrific deaths. Now Ed is definitely upset at the facts that Sam has a new love in his life and a much younger one at that. As trying to lured Sam at his place for a get together with the new person in his life could be it for a great way to kill her too. But this is how Ed is thinking to himself for motivation and see it through. Which Ed would have to act on it for a successful mishap. But Ed also thought that getting Sam along at his place could be at best because ed doesn't receive company like sam does at his home. Truthful Ed doesn't have many friends to call on. Ed was sorted of a nerd that love trains and science with a passion until he ran into liking girls. But girls didn't like poor ed back they just made fun of him and call him names. See in school Ed was a goofy looking kid with curly hair and tall without any coordination to him whatsoever. But was a honor roll student that got his lesson done. But bouncing a ball and walking at the same time he couldn't do that at all. But with an auto parts store and working for the railroad company on the side Ed is not doing bad for himself at all. With Sam buying his car parts from Ed's store is helping his dear friend sales go through the roof.

But Ed is not in any interested in Sam helping his sales that is all fine and dandy but Ed wants what matter to him is Sam's life and it's so darned hard to get it. But for sure in returned that little thing that matters to him is the women that's in Sam's life. So the inter creature has gotten june and it's need one of the other women that's in Sam's life. But Ed knows it's going to be a long and hard thing to accomplished.

Especially going for a younger woman that has a whole lot of intelligence about herself would be very difficult and complicated. When another man is around to protected that which matter most.So Mr Jekyll is the key to lureing sam to the house for Mr.Hyde is Ed's darkerside of himself to do harm and finish off that was started decades ago. But to Ed it would be worth it For thing to go back to normal. And for Sam's sake he would like for not to talk to Ed unless it's necessary. With Sam having multiple nightmares of his family and self being taunted and terrorized to death is a havoc for health issues. Now with Sam bringing Terra to the house afterwards from dinner and a walk in the park.

Sam notice the kids are still gone for the evening. So walking up on the porch Sam found a hole in the glass window in the door frame broken. But the house was dark inside so Sam called the authorities to come and to handle the situation carefully. He opens the door and found a rock on the floor with glass also.

As Sam walks throughout his home to find more damage the authorities show up on the scene. While young Terra is at the side of her boyfriend's to comfort him. As the deputy's walks throughout the house and questioning Sam about his friends and enemies but Sam told them that he doesn't know who could've done something so evil as throwing a rock through the window. By the time the deputies were done Jon and Sheila jumps out of the truck running and calling for their father to see what is going on. With a cruiser in front of the house gave both Jon and Sheila a God fearing scare there for a moment. "Hey Mr. Bentford call us if you need us again." said the deputy. "I will definitely do that." said Sam. "Dad! What in God's name happen here?" ask Jon. "Terra and I walks up on the porch. And there was a hole in the glass but no other damages." said Sam. "By the way this is Terra." said Sam. "Hello." said Jon. As Sheila looks at her like a poisonous insect that needs to be killed instantaneously before speaking. "Hi." said Sheila.

Then she walks back to her room shutting the door behind her with a queen bee atitutde. "Hello. To both of you." said Terra. "So dad what's that in your hand?" ask Jon. "The rock someone thru at the window." said Sam. "Who's in their right mind would do that dad?" ask Jon. "Wait a darn minute the deputies should've known better to take the evidence with them." said Jon. "Jon son you are absolutely right." said Sam. "I'am going to call eugene on this one." said Sam. "Now dad your prints are on that as well." said Jon. "Well let me put it down."said Sam.

As Terra looks around and wandering how come a person would just throw a stone thru someone elses window unless they had a grudge against them or the whole family.

"Is someone mad at you all?" ask Terra"Well we being having problems with a individual for a while." said Jon. As he looks at his dad while telling terra what he wants her to know. "Oh ok." said Terra. While Sam changes the subject by asking Jon about his and Sheila's evening. Because the family isn't ready to exposed the long fighting secret they have being going up against.

As Sam mentioning Sheila's name out comes Sheila from her bedroom walks strait up to Terra and ask her "Are you trying to take our father away from us?" Because you are sadly mistaking!" said Sheila. Sheila!! Stopped would you!" yelled Sam."What's her problem?" asking Terra. "You is my problem!"whore!" said Sheila. "Listen hear you big mouth b—ch! You don't know me!" said Terra. "Ladies!!! please!! stopped it!!" said Jon. "If you thinking about destroying my father b—ch! You better think again!" Slut!!" said Sheila. "That's it!! I didn't come here for this type of garb age

Sam! So if you don't shut her up! I will!" "Who you think you are talking to me like that! I don't know you and you don't know me either!" said Terra. "I don't want to know you at all!" said Sheila. "Hey!!! cool it will ya!!!" said Sam. "Sam! Take me home please!" said Terra. "I don't need this (explicit) crap! Coming from her!" said Terra.

As the evening unfold in a unusual way with a guest so mistreated in a unexpected bad language to communicate. Was never heard of until now. But was this sam's fault for bringing another woman around his family without consulting them first? Or should they accept their father's happiness and resisted later? It's not the mind that changes it's the hearts that changes. Everything flows from the heart you only say what the heart allowed you speak. But sometimes the heart is so polluted with unconscience words acts and self destruction to there isn't any room for good and love.

As Sam and Jon both trying to smooth thing over between both women is kinda differcult to do when one is demanding to go home and the other one is walking off to her room to shut the door behind her. "Hey dad that's women with a touch of attitude that can't bargain with." said Jon.

"I guess so son. I just give up." said Sam. "Shucks!" said Sam. While he go and knocks on sheila's bedroom door trying to get her to come out was impossible. "Sheila! Open this door please!" said Sam. But she wasn't breaking her silence for nothing. Sheila! Honey I need to talk to you!" so open this door now!! said sam in a angry voice. Sheila just gave her father a cold and bitter taste of silent behavior in which is the first time. As Jon talks to Terra while Sam was trying his best to talk some sense into his daughter isn't happening. "Hey dad why don't you let her be she come around." said Jon. "Terra! I'am so sorry for all this mess that my daughter has cause." said Sam. "Sam honey! You don't have to say no more I completely understand and she reminds me of my younger sister that is so spoiled." said Terra. "hahahaha!" laughing Jon. "I really thought we all should've gotten along but darn it! Sheila and her ways are like her mother's." said Sam.

As behind close doors Sheila cry herself to sleep. Thinking about Jay and the great times they shares being husband and wife. She had to go to her closet to pull out a photo album of her and Jay Jon and most of all her parents. But she had this particular photo of everybody at a church bbq. To seeing everyone's seen so happy with a joyous moment. With Jay and her mother June gone. Sheila has become so out right bitter and cold to anyone that's not family neither friends are just much more a foe then a friend. But one thing that Sheila hasn't talk about is her nightmares of Jay being kill by someone they all knew And the same person that kill her husband is the same that killed her mother. But in her dream she can't make out who the killer is. And just a week ago jon himself had a nightmares of him and his father's limb's were torned from their bodies and eaten by the creature.

And Sam has had nightmares after June's disappearance and still and steady having them persistent. So the nightmares of the innocent has giving way for evil to torched the mind. Now with the creature in everyone's head is not making the family stronger it's making them fall apart slowly.

Sorted of weak until everyone is fighting each other. But this isn't the time to lower their guards for evil and deadly destruction to move in on good grounds.

For a creature without a conscience will be glad with re assurance to do what it known to do. Is to kill!. Now for weeks there has being silence and a bit of peace for the Bentford's but didn't know when the creature would strike.

Now with a house full of prey sounds great for this predator. But not far off the predator is keeping close eyes on this house still until his destine is met by get this man of this house his way. Out in the opening when no ones around all to himself is the best way to get an enemy. So no one can intervene on the enemies behalf cry and no one can hear you. No mercy at all. But to watch your enemy cry out his soul and beggaging for mercy on his life asking for forgiveness at whatsoever that was done in the past. It's amazing how people do just that when in the presence of trouble.

And also how that person tends to cried his soul out by talking fast with stuttering and can't pronounce words correctly. But all just a few symptom of fear just to keep your soul a bit longer. Now and before there was a hard struggle involved just trying to lured Sam alone which Sam said before he does't trust Edward Dart alone. But no one will understand why not. See it does sits in the back of sam's mind that Ed wasn't trying to be his friend before until the disappearance of June coming by the house feeling sorry looking like dog crap on a stick. But to Sam it was a load of bull.

As everyone was talking there was that sound again coming from far off from the east. Coming on strong and loud the engines can be heard inside the house. Sam and Jon looks at each other for some support then they both went for their weapons. While Terra looks so suprises with a bit of curiousity. "Terra! I will explaine to you later at whats going on ok." said Sam. "Why sure."said Terra. Jon started to turned the lights out. Now Sheila to has come to help if needed. The house was dark inside with everyone ready for a fight. As the locomotives slowed down near the house but kept going pulling military cargo.

So the unexpected didn't show. But had the family on edge with a added of embarrasment in front of a house guest.

"So what's going on?"ask Terra."Well we being having a problem with a certain someone and he has terrorized us for the longest." said Sam. "And it shows up unexpectedly for some damn reason here to attack."said Sam."Wow really?" ask Terra. "Have you all tried to get the sheriff involved?" ask Terra. "Haha the sheriff! Shuck's his ass is not going to do a thing but keep taking tax payers money that's what he will keep doing." said Sam. "Him and that sorry deputy." said jon. Sheila looks at Terra and rolled her eyes and went back to her bedroom shutting the door behind her. "She's really a hard person to get alone I take it?" ask Terra. "No she's like her mother June didn't care for other women as much." said Sam."Just give her a moment to get use to you then she would come around." said Jon.

"I'am a likable person when you get to know me right Sam!?" ask Terra. "Sheila always has being like that if you ask me." said Jon. "Well I wish she would changes her ways just for once." said Sam. As everyone was talking of Sheila's situation there was a sudden scream coming from Sheila's bedroom. As both Sam and Jon ran to rescue her from harm. Sam opens Sheila's bedroom door to find her in her bed with a pillow over her face. "Sheila! What happen?" ask sam. While Jon standing at the foot her bed with his gun loaded and ready to shoot anything that moves. And Terra looks on with more curiousity then frightening. "I just saw that damn thing looking in on me with those red eyes." said Sheila. As Jon takes off running outside to see if he can see that darn creature again near the house. So Jon will have a reason to shoot something but no signs of the creature's whereabouts. But Jon walks towards the corn field where it's is tremendously dark from where he is standing to the railroad tracks. By Jon walking a little further over in the corn field he heard something walking towards him and fast. "Stop! Or i'll shoot!!" said Jon. The eyes the smell and the height was right there with Jon. THUD! The creature knocks Jon on his butt but Jon retaliates with a shot as quickly before the creature could do anymore damage. Now sam has show up to rescue Jon from being a victim. The creature takes off towards the darkest part of the corn field to camouflage himself from anymore slugs to his body parts.

"Jonny!!!" yells Sam. "Over here dad!!" said Jon. "Are you alright?" ask sam. "I think so. I think it might have cut me with it's talons." said jon. "That son of a b—ch!!" said Sam.

Jon was bleeding but doesn't know where at as both Sam and jon headed back to the house to check on Sheila and Terra but Jon kept looking back towards the tracks to see if the engine was near or maybe hear it. But neither one so in Jon's head that creature whereabouts are close by. That's very odd not to see the locomotive afterwards. Because after a confrontational the creature runs to it's engine for safety.

But this time it runs to the thick of the darkness for cover and knowning a weapon was at hand. By being wounded before the creature has sense to know to strike and then move for cover. But Jon did misses the target again. By the way Jon is thinking that the creature is near the house.

There isn't no mistake about it to know somethings is different about how this creature keeps on re-appearing in different ways to strike. How and when is the issue. "Wait! A freakin minute! Dad look can we put some lamps out here so we can see it coming?" ask Jon. "Well Jonny that's a great ideal to know and to do but we need to run power from the house to out here." said Sam. The darkness is a temporary uses for the creature to use. It has capabilties to make itself invisible also but can't disgusted the smell of it's body.

So it's part of it's nature the smell comes with the evil and taste of wickeness. By being in content of killing makes it very satisfied with it's prey and appetite for destroying. As for the Bentford men there is a counter act to this situation for a craving act to kill harm or no danger in killing a man like beast. But this creature has prolong it's death for the longest where something has to give. For what matter is no one else is to get harm or hurt. But by the laws and physics there isn't any way around danger itself but to be careful at all times.

It's kinda hard to do when everyone is so blind sided at the time of leisure. But it seens that the time when the crea ture is at it's best when no one is expecting it. As Sam and Jon has taking the initiative to put up lights out near the corn field to see who's coming and going but one little discretional the creature may have is make itself invisible to it's prey without knowning. With the next strike could be a deadly attack.

View of Discretion
Chpt XII

The evening was far spent for fun and laughter but also to mend each other with respect and understanding. Now as Sheila make her way to the kitchen to where Terra decides to follow Sheila into the kitchen to talk to her. But Sheila just ignored her. "Can I talk to you for a moment please?" ask Terra. "Look Sheila i'm not here to make your life miserable or cause problems but to be a friend to you and Jon." said Terra. Suddenly Sheila turns to Terra and ask her an unthinkable question. "Really! Why are you here!?" ask Sheila. "If you want to make peace with me! Stop seeing my father for starters!" said Sheila. As she went back to her room and slammed the door behind her. As Terra just stood there for a moment thinking that Sheila is a undepicable b—ch and acting childish and inconsiderate.

But Terra just place the F word on her for Forgettable and nonsense to go on. After the two death's in the family Sheila hasn't being the same. Lost mom June then her husband Jay was taken from her in a weird way. But at the end of the day she still has her father and brother for protection and no one else. Sheila is thinking of the worse that can happen in the relationship of her father and young girlfriend can be a total disaster for her to see coming a mile away but Sheila did warned Terra of the consequences and reprecussion that can occur if her father is done wrong in any kinda way. While in the kitchen just sitting around the table talking of a plan to catch this creature is to follow it to it's place of hiding that's near by. Sam Jon and Terra are in deep conversation about ways to catch this thing and kill it. But sam notice that Terra is showing interested in helping with there situation while Sheila wants to exclude herself from everyone. That's not family to her.

As the night winds down with everyone getting tired and headed for bed. Now Jon insist on staying up a little longer then usual with terra watching him from far off. Down and deep inside of Terra's heart she is starting to have feeling's for her older boyfriend son. But not to show anything Which is so wrong on her behalf but it's natural to have feeling's for someone on the same page as you are. But being very discretional is a good way to keep thing in order then having things in a chaotic swing then comes mayhem between couples then drag family members on board. Now the world knows all they need to know about you and yours.

So meanwhile Sam ask Terra to stay the night with him insteaded of going home. It's very late to be traveling by herself because no woman wants to be out late by herself without a man being with her. As Terra said yes to spending the night in her mind would be a great thing to keep watch on Jon's every moves without sam suspecting anything. "Sure baby cakes I would love to stay the night." said Terra.

"Dad she can stay in my room for the night." said Jon.

"I'll take the sofa in the meantime." said Jon with a grin.

Well Sam isn't to happy with the sleeping arrangements that he just heard from Jon and Terra agreed to it. Sam would like his young girlfriend to lay with him for pleasure and ease things that's on his mind. So Sam approach Terra to see if she could change her mind in coming with him but she was already in the bed tuck away. As Jon was in the kitchen for a midnight snack with a coldcut sandwich and a taste of beer in his favor mug. As sitting down to enjoy it.

Sam walks in with a dirty look and something to say to his son. "Jonny you talks too damn much." said Sam.

"what!?" ask Jon. "Dad what are you talk about?" ask Jon.

"you know what i'am talking about don't play stupid with me son." said Sam. "Cmon Dad seriously! You are mad because I let her sleep in my bed and not with you?" ask Jon.

"You are ridiculous." said Jon. "If you even think about touching her Jonny I promise you trouble son." said Sam.

"And you listen to me dad! I don't want your girlfriend she isn't my type first of all." said Jon. "That's good to know son." said Sam. "Goodnight Jon." said Sam. But Jon didn't reply he just look away from his father.

But not knowing that both Sheila and Terra both heard the men talking. As Terra play as she was sleeping but eavesdropping at the same time. And knows she is the subject that the men are talking about. For sure she wants Jon in a way that only she can imagine. Now Sheila had her room door crack to listen to what was said. As listening she started to feel that anger spirit come over her that she needs to nip this thing in the butt. Sheila knows how women tentive to create problems between family members. Like Terra is doing now. In Sheila's mind. Sheila will deal with Terra later on tomorrow quick and easy. "I'am not going to tolerate this situation any longer." said Sheila. Thinking to herself as she sat down on the side of her bed. Asking herself, "What needs to be done?" thought Sheila.

While Jon was still in the kitchen sitting there thinking how his father would think that he would mess with his girlfriend like he is a idiot. Who would come at their children like that?

And then tell them that there is going to be trouble. So sitting there thinking here comes trouble herself walks into the kitchen and reach for a glass to get a drink of water. But as she reach for the glass Jon looks at her like a lost pup.

She came into the kitchen in a see through gown with white panties on and nothing more. The gown that once belongs to Mrs. June. Sam has givin to Terra to sleep in.But if Sheila would see another woman in her mother's garment she would have a fitting rage.

As Jon sat and gaze at Terra's beautiful body while she was sipping on a glass of water. With tendency came to his mind of laying with her. But reality quickens him to remeember what his father had told him hours ago. If he would tried to touch Terra in any formal or fashionable way there would be trouble between him and his father. With Terra standing there: has open thee eyes of Jon. Now Jon hasn't seen a woman in years but Terra could make him see for days on days with the love and affection spilling all over between them both. But the gown that Terra has on made Jon realize in what he has being missing for a long period of time. Terra will always be stuck in the back of Jon's mind. Also could this be the night that Terra could give Jon a night to take in remembrance of her for nights to come?

Or would Jon like to reckeon with his father for crossing that line?

With jon in a small hypnosis from gaze at Terra's well being:Sam yelled for Terra. "Terra!" Sam calls."In here in the kitchen getting me some water." said Terra. And as she leaves the kitchen she whispers in Jon's ear. "Sweet dreams Jon."said Terra. As she went to see what Sam wants. Jon is in the kitchen still wandering in what just happen. Because for a moment Jon thought real hard not to touch her but being a man with testosterones chromosomes and hormones that's what happens when in love with a person that's doesn't belong to you. In which is call covetness with lust on the other end helping the man's thoughts. That's from both participate in sharing something that is consensual that set things apart in a silent way. Not knowing the vulnerability that they would put a person like Sam through.

Now Jon knows that hurting his father could damage their relationship. But Jon has a made up mind to test the waters to see where it may take him. As the night unfolds Jon gets ready to lay down on the sofa to get comfortable and get some sleep.And as soon as jon started to remove his shoes he heard a train coming from the west so Jon had put his shoes back on. And went to the back door to see if anything would look suspicious or all out of the ordinary. Then Sam appeared also looking and ready. But Jon just stay his distants from his father in the presence of Terra. As of now the game has being changed cause of a woman's appearance.

Now it's seems like a collision course is set for a father & son duel with weapons at hand. And the winner recieves the woman's love for good. But Sam do loves his son and will not think of harming him in no way. The same as well with Jon will not harm or put his dad at risk. But when you see two boy's fighting over the same apple that can be a ridiculous way of show love towards one another. A apple can be split down the middle for sharing but a woman or a girl on thee other hand is known for treading on thin ice perhaps.

Well another false alarm the train kept moving going east pulling freight and moving with power. Sam and Jon just looked at one another without saying a word they both resume where they left from doing. While both Sheila and terra stay in the back out of harms way. Trying to stay safe as possible by letting the men do in what's needed. To protect the them and the house. Sam went back to his bedroom but on his way back to his room he stop to check on Terra especially to see how she is holding up.Then he came to Sheila door and knock to see if she was ok but she didn't answer. So Sam assume she was still sleep so he went on into his room. Sheila wasn't sleep she was still going through a thing with Terra being in the house.

Now it's very late and Sam is knockout by snorting with the covers move to one side of the bed. And Jon was out also like a light but he was feeling a hand on his right leg so he open his eyes to see what's going on. "Damn." said Jon. It's Terra getting ready to create a problem by lying with him in a dark house. The mood was just right with the fireplace warming things as everyone else was sleeping as Jon roll over on his back to see whats in store with Terra decides to climb on top of him with Jon allowing something that is so pleasant and trying not to fight this wonderful feeling of a woman's touch. As Jon can't help himself but to let things run it's course that could cause conflict between him and his father later on. To Jon feeling good can only happen once if you allowed it.

As everything was transpiring inside the creature was steps away from carrying out it's deadliest attack every on this innocent family. The house was quite warm inside and quiet with the fireplace lighted the livingroom up. While Jon just lying still on his back soon enough he started to touch Terra at the waist. Then Jon started undressing Terra then Terra would do the same to Jon now both are naked then kissing and heavy breathing. Now that love had exposed itself between the two individual's there will be consequesences and a little of reprecussions afterwards. Just like sin then comes death. Have fun now then the punishment.

There will be counter acts all through life. "No no no we shouldn't be doing this." said Jon. "uh uuh c'mon Jonny lets finish for what we have gotten started." said Terra. "I won't say a word if we could finsh this." said Terra. As Jon grabs her and holds on to her for pleasure Jon lays with Terra that this is a night to remember forever. For the passion with each other has molded into a mountain of hiden love and a lots of hurt ahead.

So Terra has gotten her a fixed before the night was over with Jon on thee other hand will have a heart of heaviness as burdens starts to mount for him for being disobedient to his father and his unfaithfulness as well. As the sexual feeling continues with hugging and holding each other tightly at this point there isn't anything that can separate them now.

With a weird and funny feeling of tingling as he sticks to Terra like glue to paper the feelings has gotten so strong it was hard to separate when all of your brain is else where.

But if Sam could've caught them in the act then it would've have being a painful separation among Jon and Terra. And so much hurt for Sam to have to see all that betrayal happening right in front of his face. As Sam was sleeping with all this was going on. And now that the love making is over and done with Jon has told Terra that she is his girlfriend now. But Terra just looks into Jon's baby blue's and said "I love you Jonny." But Jon didn't reply to that. It just hit him like a ton of bricks with reality has kicked in knowningly that he just messed up by having intercourse with his father's girlfriend. But while all of this was going on sheila has heard all that was said to the love making and to terra telling Jon that she love him. As Sheila tips toe back to her room without being seen by either Jon or Terra. But once Sheila has returned to her room Sheila started to cry for her dad's hurt.

"That b—ch I told her if she messes up I will have her no good ass." said Sheila. "I can't believe this sh--." said Sheila. "She just wait until I get my hands on her narrow ass."said Sheila. Well Sheila was quite upset with what she had heard and saw as well. So therefore she doesn't know to tell her dad about everything or to blackmail her brother and whip the crap out of Terra. The next few days is hell in the Bentford's home. The morning has arrived and Sam is getting up in good spirit and full of energy. That he may do something nice with Terra and his kids.

But jon was still asleep on the sofa as sam walks into the livingroom then the kitchen. "Hey Jonny! Morning! Are you going to sleep your life away?" ask Sam. When Jon decides to turn over to look at the coffee table he notice there were a pair of white panties on the floor between him on the sofa and coffee table. Jon was hysterical and hope that his father didn't see that at all. So when Sam went into the kitchen to make coffee Jon grabs the underwear and hid them under the sofa As he sat down to think about lastnights love making could ruin his relationship with his dad so to keep peace between him and his dad is to do what it takes to keep things from getting out of hand. But Jon still has a made up mind to see Terra again or more often then suspected. Oh boy! What a way to hurt someone you love so deep and dearly. After everything had went down from the previous night is still lingering in the back of Jon's mind until he can't focus now on the world.

As the day is started in a weird and bitter way Sheila comes through the livingroom looking at her brother with a dirty and disrespectful look. "Morning Sheila!" said Jon. But she didn't reply to Jon as she ignored him to talk to her father in the kitchen. So Jon got up to ease into the kitchen to hear at what was said. "Good morning Dad how are you this morning?" ask Sheila. As she gave her brother a stare like she can cut his neck off from his body. Or shoot him with his owned gun. "Morning sweetie it seems that you are in a great mood this morning what you got enough rest? i hope you did." ask Sam.

"I guess Terra is still sleeping."said Sam."i see some people had a good night last night." said Sheila. As Jon looks at his sister in a scared and surprising stare until Terra walks into the kitchen as well. "Good morning to all." said Terra. As she gives a wink to Jon especially. But she go over to Sam to give him a kiss on the lips and immediately Jon removed himself from their presence. Walking into the livingroom looking guilty with a agitated attitude. And knowning deep down inside that Terra belongs to him now. As Sheila do the same by going back to her room to get dress to go to the mall. Whatsoever everyone was doing in the house was stop at the sound of the train that coming up the tracks and stop behind the house. Because of the dwarf signal is lit in red. Now everybody had grab their weapons of war just in case something may feel froggy and leap. As everyone gather at the windows and the back door looking to see what is about to transpired over on the tracks.

But while Jon was standing at the kitchen window Terra walks by him and pinch Jon on his butt. Jon immediately gave her a dirty look cause one she leaves her underwear on the floor in the livingroom for sam to see. Then she kisses Sam like nothing ever happened. As Jon's mind is taking a whirl of questions and putting them in perpective for answers on where do he also stands in Terra's life now.

Now as the locomotive's starts to move out slowly pulling freight and automobile's behind it to the next county. But Sam was ready for a fight today. With Terra by his side and Jon on the other. Sheila cover the front door just in case.

Again the family and friend works together to save each other from the evil and wicked tracks. Sam was in a great mood all day long and Jon neither Sheila wanted to interruppted his spirit with words of dishonest and truthful. So the best way is to give their father plenty of room to enjoy his days of happiness. Because this day could be his very last. With that said Sheila kept her tattling to herself with the hopes of kicking Terra's ass all over Lajunta. Jon stays out of the way of his father until he figured a way to spilled the truth to him. Well Terra is still wants to see Jon at her leisure. But the next few weeks will be like a camp of hell.

With a touch of chaos and battling a side order of wicked is a feast for war: with death at the finish line waiting on the one to fall first and from it's sting. But the Bentford's has had so many victories over this creature of evil and wickeness and now stuff and confusion in the family. But when a family like the Bentford's this is how love fits tight without evil partaking whatsoever. Now Sheila has approach her brother to confront him on his wrong doings with Terra in the kitchen with their father. "Jonny how could you do this to dad?" ask Sheila while whispering to her brother.

"What are you talking about?" ask Jon. "You know what the hell i'am talking about so don't play stupid with me Jonny." said Sheila. "Sheila will you leave me the hell alone?" ask Jon. "Don't let dad find out about this." said Sheila.

"Oh yes you owe me." said Sheila. "So! You blackmailing me now?" ask Jon. "Look here! You will keep your mouth shut because you don't know nothing." said Jon. "I know more then you think I know." said Sheila. "your lying!" said Jon. "O if i'm lying then did it feel good having sex with your father's girlfriend?" ask Sheila. Jon didn't know what exactly to say or to expect. Now jon's life has taken a twist in a direction he didn't expected to go. But Jon's consceince is crying out loud for him to reveal the truth to his father. The truth is always welcome into the bentford's home if nothing else the truth is absolutely gets the respect then a lie. So Jon needs to be on point when he reveal the truth about him and Terra. Because Jon knows it will save his life from heartaches and causing embarrasment pain for his father especially and himself. With grief lie's and cheated on isn't a way of accepting love from those who are trying to give it.

Will Sam be able to forgive Jon for his actions on being disobedient to him? Some people would have forgave right away. But there is a punishment coming for to rough things out to have those same things much smoother ahead. But in the mean while the Bentford's are about to receive a unwanted guest to make things rougher then they are. It's a cool and sunny day to where the air is flowing down from the rockies to make the fall setting just right this time of the year. But everything seens to go bad when Edward Dart decides to show up on the doorstep of the Bentford's home. Ed claiming that he should pay a visit a little more often then usual. But Sam doesn't need anymore problems showing up unannounce visitors just to seek the Bentford's business for town gossip to thrive on. The thing is that Ed's body healed tremendously. It's like he went and did a body transformation to where he is not limping anymore and has a much more decietfulness attitude as well. So with him coming to seek out what to find and place an attack on the new version of June's so called replacement. Was well thought of: "Hey Sam." said Ed. "What's up my friend?" ask Sam. "I thought I should stop and see hows things are holding up for you all around here." said ed. "Well! Awful without June not here." said Sam. AsTerra reappeared from the back bedroom to where Sam was she walks over to Ed and introduce herself to Ed. "Hi i'm Terra." said Terra. "Well i'm Edward Dart a friend of the family but you can call me Ed." said Ed. "It's an honor to meet you." said Ed. "Well Jonny is a lucky man to have you." said Ed. Immediately Sam was offended and had an attitude with Ed for being so nosey. "Sorry Sam I just thought she was with Jonny." said Ed.

"No you nosey of a man she is my lady and stop looking at her like you are doing and close your darn mouth!" said Sam. "Sorry! I better get going for someone turned very bitter with me." said Ed. "Really! Ed what in the heck did you come over here for?" ask Sam. "Seriously Sam I just stopped to see how you all were doing and let you know that I was thinking about you all." said Ed. "Ok! You seen that we are doing quite well other then that bye Ed." said Sam. "Ok Sam i'am leaving." said Ed. Now as Ed is leaving and pulled the front door shut he had a bitterly look and a bit of a transformation on the porch of the Bentford's house to going back inside to do his attack especially on sam and terra both but not knowing where the other two are at in the house. "I'am going to get you soon enough sam and your little girlfriend." said Ed. "You S.O.B" said Ed.

With his eyes turning colors from the raging evil and wicked entity inside that is burning to get out. But Ed must try to tame it with a good thought and not bad. As getting into his car Ed has a plan to get Sam alone to destroyed him and come back to wipe out the whole family if necessary.

So what Ed wanted to do was to get his so called friend to come alone over to his house to look at his car. Then to have sam to come inside for a drink for old time sake and not knowing that drink is drug with a sleeping cocktail to make Sam as drowsy as could be. Enough to do damage to his hated enemy more less to kill him. But Ed must fix his car to where it's not running properly. That's the wicked thought that Ed had in mind to be carried out in the next day of so. And Ed is also thinking where to hide his engne when the day come for sam to drop by to look at his vehicle.

See the same railroad tracks that runs behind sam's home is the same tracks that runs by Ed's home also. On the side of Ed's place are two sets of tracks and then trees and woods.

So when Ed is in his creature state he can get up high into those trees to see what's going on at the Bentford's house.

Ed can see the family comings and goings with his wicked vision he has. That is one of the capabilties that comes with the evil traits he has taken on. As Ed is pulling up into his driveway he noticed that Sheila passes his home and as he waves to her but Sheila looks and kept going.

That evens anger Ed in a way to go after her and he did.

Every turn she made Ed did follow. But she never notice that Ed was on her tail like a cat chases a mouse. But Ed has figured if he could only get sheila to talk to him. That would be enough to get close to her for to grab her and take her hostage.

Finally sheila pulls up into the shopping center parking lot to check on a deal on a dress that she was looking for. But she waited for it to go on sale. Therefore she still hasn't noticed that Ed is still in pursuit of her. With him parking a couple of stalls over from her to make it possible to do what needs to be done by luring her into his car. If he could just get close enough to get to her to get to sam and then others that could be the way of getting his evil and wicked deeds done. But Sheila kinda made things a little impossible for what Ed had in mind. With other citizens around and out in thee opening he couldn't put on a show by grabing her with everyone else witness to what happens.

So Ed insisted on waiting for her to reach her vehicle then he would grab her with a clothe full of a knockout solution to put her out like a baby. And then back to his place they go. Now that Sheila is inside the mall to go where she need to find the same dress she saw in the newspaper that was on sale. Get it and go. But only one thing that got her attention was shoes. Sheila couldn't resist from looking at all styles that caught her eyes. So why not indulge. As women all have to have a nice dress they might as well have the shoes to go with it. Styling and profiling is the name of ones games. Sheila is like most women's is to look their very best to catch a guy eyes. And not only that but to look beautiful period. Another problem was that Sheila departed from another exit door to get to her car. While Ed sat in his car and didn't know that Sheila has returned to her vehicle that quickly. Well he missed her again as she pulls out of the stall she was in she notice that there was a car pulling out at the same time she was. And the car just stop in back of her for no apparent reason. Sheila looks in her rear view mirror to see what's going on then she looked and what a surprised. It's Ed. Sheila rolls her window down to see what he wanted of course he tried to get her out of her car.

But she wouldn't move a lick from her seat. "Hi Sheila I thought I bump into you." said Ed. "I don't think you did Mr. Dart it doesn't feel like we touch vehicles." said Sheila.

Then there was a stare down between Ed and Sheila Ed was still in a persuasive way by trying to lure Sheila outta her car. But she told Ed that she was in a hurry she had to be else where at 5:30 and close her door and speed off. Once again Ed's timid and spineless ways aren't getting him what he desires most is a victim. Now standing there and getting angry by the minute he choose to followed her and run her off the road before she could make it home. Now Sheila is about fifteen minutes from the house when she spotted Ed in her rear view mirror directly on her tail at the traffic light. Then Ed slightly bump her then he lost control and started pushing her into on coming traffic. As Sheila couldn't stopped another car T bone her. As Sheila was a little unconscience with her head scrape and bleeding As innocent bystanders and other drivers take initiative to see if everyones was alright. One driver told Sheila not to move and lay still until the paramedic's arrive. Ed walks over to Sheila's car to get her out of the mangle vehicle so he can take her with him but so many people were standing around and watching Ed's every move. By the time paramedic's has rush to the scene Ed had to leave the scene quickly because someone had pointed in his direction that he is the culprit that cause the accident.

While trying to leave the scene a deputy stops Ed near his car to questioning him on the accident. "Sorry officer my foot slip and hit the accelerator instead of the brake." "By the way I know her." said Ed. "Just don't go no where." said the deputy. Now and therefore Ed is trying to leave the scene without being notice after the deputy told him not to leave. But Ed is trying to leave any way. Meanwhile back at the Bentford's residences they aren't aware of the accident that Sheila is in. As Jon getting ready to walk out the front door to get into his truck the deputy's had the dis patched to call Sam to notify him of Sheila's situation and her whereabouts. "Hello this is Sam." "What in God's name happen?" ask Sam. Sam drops the phone the minute he was told of Sheila's situation. Sam runs outside to tell Jon the news that Sheila was involved in a accident. "Jon we need to run to the hospital." said sam. "Dad what's going on?" asking Jon. "Oh God! Sheila had a accident." said Sam. "Dad is she ok?" ask Jon. As Sam and Terra all climb into the truck to go and see Sheila not a word was said between the three of them. As everyone's minds is thinking of Sheila is ok nothing minor. And at the scene of the accident Ed was held for questioning on what cause the accident. While sitting in the back of the deputy cruiser;

Ed was starting to show signs of transfigurate with one of his eyes turned red and the other one was grey. One of his hands was hairy with the talons are starting to reappear.

When looking at Ed you would think he had a touch of heterochromia iridis but no that's the evil that wants that need to be release. The side of Jekyll and Hyde. But Ed is trying his best to control the entity that's inside that needs to be release and soon. If so the creature could kill the deputy and destroyed the cruiser in the process. But before Ed can turned into a dreadful creature the deputy decides to let Ed go after he gave his statement on the accident. Soon as Ed was release he runs to a abandon building to get out of sight before being discovered by the citizens of lajunta and definitely no attention from the law enforcement stand point.

Once Ed get his evil half in control then he can make his way back to his car to leave. And find out whereabouts is Sheila and which way the e.m.p's took her. Now Ed is in a nerves stake. Because of his actions he must face his enemy like a creature in disguise or more like a wolf in sheeps skin to concealed it's true identity. But the day of reckeoning may come soon enough for those who can't control it's entity. "Excuse me officer. Where and which way did the paramedic's go?" ask Ed. "I believed they are taking her to Lajunta Mermorial." said the deputy. "Thank you." said Ed. Now departing from the deputy that officer was lookat Ed's in a unusual and awful way. As going throughout the crowd to get to his car he noticed that everyone was gazing at him for some reason. But when returned to his vehicle he looks into his rear view mirror and what did he see? He had half of his face was revealed that's why the crowd was acting and looking disturbing. The creature was exposed a bit which hurt Ed in a unusual way. Ed's face was disfigure from holding the evil inside and not releasing it when need to.

As the saying go's whatsoever is done in the darkness will eventually come to the light. With these special traits of evil Ed wasn't careful at all for what he wish for and now it's fighting his insides needed to get out at once. Instead of going to his place he decides to go over to the hospital to see if he can get Sheila still. But seems not able to get close to her so Ed turned around to go on home. But thinking about coming back later to get her for his hostage to get to Sam alone. With his face looking the way it is was kinda hard to walk into a hospital and ask for help and looking half man and the other half was a murderous creature. Trying to come back at a later hour would be best. To get her.

The Enemy Grounds

Chpt XIII

Meanwhile Sam Jon and Terra has shown up in a panic way trying to get some answers on the accidents. And Sheila's whereabouts and who to talk too. "Hi my daughther is here and her name is Sheila Bentford Silas." said Sam. "Yes she is in with the doctors they will be out to let you know what's going on."said the nurse. As Sam Terra and Jon grab seats in the waiting area to wait and see what's going on.

Until Sam started to be impatient by cussing and can't sit still.

So worried about Sheila's well being until everyone seems to snap at each other for no apparent reason. Sam said something ridiculous to Jon then Jon does the same back to his dad. AsTerra sit's and looks at Jon with a sneeky smile thinking about what her and Jon has done by sharing a moment together but Jon isn't paying any attention to her with his mind on his sister's well being. With a bit of a tention building up between Sam and Jon to where both men are about to lose their cool towards one another. Because of a young woman has come between them. One is very feisty and very jealous if another man looks at her. With the other thinks she belongs to him especially after having to commit adultry in his father's house.

But meantime Ed has show up at the hospital's back entrance to keep from being regconized. Ed knows he can't walk all over the building to look for Sheila's whereabouts and not get caught. So he do the unthinkable. "Excuse me where is the front desk?" ask Ed. "Go through the double doors and you are there." said the nurse. Not knowing just a few feet away is the family. Therefore Ed has made several unsucceessful attempts to getting what he is craving for like a shark that tasted blood and need more of it. And at this time Ed the creature and half man and half beast be on point this time with no mistakes.

Ed made it to the front desk asking about Sheila's whereabouts and which way to her room. Ed walks into the room of Sheila and not thinking of the mess he has cause.

But to take her without being notice. But Sheila was heavy sedative to cause her to be more sleepiness. So this is a way for Ed to capitalize on the situation more less have the advantage of her weakness. So it makes it harder for her to defended herself against him. Now Ed is trying to lift Sheila over his shoulder to get her out of the room he has her up and near the door checking the hallways and see who is around. But no one is around so Ed makes it's to the nearst stairwell to get to the low levels to get out of the hospital without the both of them being notice.

Meanwhile Sam Terra and Jon are waiting to go in to see if Sheila is alright. But have to get the clearence from the doctor first before headed in. And not aware that Sheila is no longer in her room. But was taken from under beneath their noses. Another situation to the family tributlations but more so the doctor has come out with great news that can comfort everyone thought's on Sheila's health and well being. "Hi i'am Doctor Loos Your daughter Sheila is very healthy and strong person. I'll keep her overnight to run some more tested." said doctor Loos. "Yes you all may go in to see her." said the doctor. As Sam leads the way into to Sheila's room that Sheila wasn't in her bed so they thought she was in the restroom but Terra looks in there and no Sheila. So everyone started to look at each other for a second to wandering if they appeared in the wrong room but was in the right room after all.

As Sam trying to find a nurse and ask to see if anyone seen his percious Sheila? "Oh my God where in the heck! could she be?" asking Jon. The hospital's security is being notify at once to check all over for the patient's whereabouts. As started to loose his cool by yelling at the nurse for not watching his sister closely. "How in the f#*K! Can you loose a patient in a hospital!?" ask Jon. "Jonny! Calm down!"said Sam. "Hey! They could have move her to another floor we wait and see what happens next." said Sam. Now on the low level of the building is Ed with Sheila over his shoulder carrying her to his car to get out of there as quickly as possible. Without being notice as putting Sheila into his car Ed notice that security is running rampant for some reason. But didn't care. All he wanted was Sheila for Sam later. See he needs Sheila for a even trade for her dad. If Ed can get Sheila he can lured sam into his evil web to kill him for all the hurt that he put Ed through. So now Ed has something that is so precious to him and what is Sam so willing to pay for to get her back is the question? Oh of course Sam will give his life for both of his children. Sam is a man that isn't laying down to this situation or let thing's blow over and call it quits. Sam lost his wife now he has to loose his daughther!? No way in heck Sam isn't putting up with this at all. It's hard to show humbleness when it come to the family. That's when lines are cross and things need to be corrected and quickly. As the hospital's staff and security alike running around a huge structure of Lajunta Memorial could be very frustrated if not knowing where to go or to look for someone can be awfully frustrating. But looking for sheila's whereabouts is a piece of work. No one seems to know where this patient is.

Now the local authority has being notify to come in to assist the hospital's security team on this matter. But while all this is going on the father and brother demanded answers from the hospital's staff. On how can a patient that is heavy sedative get up and walk out? To Sam and Jon none of this makes any sense at all. Further down cornway road is the car of the kipnapper himself with Sheila's helpless body in the trunk of Ed's beat up junker. As he rides pass the home of Sheila's to get to his place. Ed moves quick to get his victim inside before being discovered by nosey neighbor's.

As opening the trunk Ed looks around to see who was in sight before lifting sheila's helpless body outta the trunk.

But no one is in sight. With Sheila still heavy sedated from the medication she started to ask question about "why is it so cold?" Sheila wasn't dress when Ed removed her from her room. All she had was a hospital's gown and underwear on. So Ed took her as she was to get out of harms way. Ed was kinda excited to carried out his plan to get what he also deserved and that is respect. "Alright come my dear girl." said Ed. Now up the three steps into the house of Ed's as he act a bit nerves getting his keys for to get inside before someone notice them.

Now getting Sheila out of the cold trunk of his car causes her to have hypothermia a bit from the cold wind from the mountains. Ed slightly lays sheila on sofa and covered her from the cold house. But Ed went to grab some rope to tied Sheila's hands and feet together so no resisting can go on.

Then he steps out back on the porch to grab a few logs for the fireplace. Why he notice the sun was almost down then he glance at his locomotive wandering if he should fire it up to go and sit behind Sam's house. But first he has to attend to Sheila first by restraining her before her meds ware off.

While getting the rope prepared to rope her feet together Ed stood over Sheila helpless young and beautiful body just observing her in a sense of having someone like her in his life. To wake up to everyday and enjoy life together and also a family as well. But the evil inside is telling him other things to think of as killing her. But Ed doesn't want Sheila he needs Sam instead. Ed's work is halve done and soon will be accomplish once he get sam and release Sheila. A even trade is what's it call. A him for her. As Ed was roping Sheila's hands together. Sheila started to come to and asking Ed "Why are you doing this?" ask Sheila. Ed just looked at her like he was dumb founded. But kept quiet about everything. NowSheila started to cried and scream."Heeeelp!!!" said Sheila. "Hey damn it!! keep it down!!!" said Ed. "I need for your father to come and get you if he wants you back." said Ed. "Your freakin father has being a thorn in my side all these years." said Ed. "I say it's time to settled the damn score!" said Ed. As Sheila try to work the ropes on her hands and feet. "Now you are going to listen to me baby girl and stop all your screaming and sit still!" said Ed. "If you don't I will throw your beautiful ass in a cold basement tried me!!" said Ed. "Let the spiders and the big bugs crawl all over you!" said Ed.

"Mr. Dart again why are you doing this?" ask sheila. "Your father has taken something from me that was so precious and now I can't never get it back not ever!" said Ed. "Well what did he supposely took from you?" ask Sheila. "Shut!

The hell up!!" said Ed. "You don't need to know my business!" said Ed. Sheila looks at him in a frightening way that she can see that Ed face is starting to look familiar to her. But never thought where has she seen his face with the eyes and that smell starts to bring a message to her mind.

With his back turned Ed was transforming right in front of sheila As the evil side starts to come about with Sheila was afraid to see and watch she close her eyes and fainted.

It was a awful thing to see as a young girl that was scared out of her wits to witness ed a mindless individual before the creature state has take over. But meanwhile back at the hospital as security team and law enforcement all alike are calling it a night on searching for Sheila's whereabouts. So the next thing is to put a statewide search for to find Sheila.

Therefore Sam is acting his age and very fiesty with all the hospital's staff as well as Jon. As terra trying to keep peace among both men. But for the simple facts Terra is enjoying this masquerade that is surrounding Sheila's whereabouts.

As Terra put it's that she never like Sheila in the beginning but now she has a heart for understanding that Sheila is a well spoiled brat that got her way in everything there is.

But hopes nothing happens to her. Women are alike in the ways of thinking. By going from hate to loveable to each other. Feelings are a big part of all women's lives. Like the society today we must accept our weaker points as well as the stronger points as well with men mad at things and a woman mad at other people and the beast of the earth is mad at everyone accept it's self. It's funny how life is dealt wouldn't you say? Presumably so and how to look at life through a lens. If not to complicated then try being content to way things are. Now with a statewide search going on the sheriff's office was notify at first. Because that's county responsibility to do a thorough search from one side to another. To cover every inch of the state of colorado. As sheriff Protzman shows up on the scene but sam wasn't in no mood to talk too. But sheriff did his best on June's disappearance but still very little evidents on her case. And that's why the bitterness that sam is showing towards the law. "Hi Sam I know it's being a minute since we talk to each other but I can respect that you are still mad at the force for not finding your wife but believed me it wasn't enough evidents to go on looking." said the sheriff.

"Sheriff only thing I have to say to you is you must find my daughther!." said Sam. "And another thing if that was your wife would you stop looking for her?" ask Sam. As sheriff Protzman looks surprisely shock at the question that was thrown at him. Made him realized that Sam was absolutely right of course he wouldn't given up so easy. He would put a a.p.b. Out to look very intense to comb every corner of the country for his wife who he love so dearly.

But for Sam he was just to forget about his wife and accepted life as is. It's very ironic when the government figure heads and law officials alike. Shows very little concerned about the victims situation until the very same situation hits home then they wants to rub out the whole planet for crying aloud. For a great example is a law officer can shoot your child and be acquited. Until his own is shot by someone that is on the same force as himself. That's when the precinct is a kingdom that is divided a entity harms itself. Because all of the government usually stick together when destroying others as in humanity. So Sam isn't alone for caring for his family so much until he finds out about his son and young girlfriend has being doing behind his back and when he is asleep. He doesn't know a thing not as yet. But Jon does love his father as much as missing his mother with great respect. And now the family has seen it share of casualties from June's disappearance Sheila's husband Jay taken and killed and now Sheila is nowhere to be found. As Sam was sitting in the lobby next to Terra and across from Jon he looks at Jon with a disturbing look to make hairs stand up on the back of the neck. "Jonny! I hate to said it but our creature is back." said Sam. But Jon just looks at his dad in a way that is unusual before saying anything. "Dad how do you know this?" ask Son. "Shucks! Son something just isn't right about my daughter and your sister damn it!" said Sam.

Finally a little light is being shine on the situation. One of the guards had the audacity to rewind some of the tapes of previous night to see what happen to Sheila's whereabouts.

But in some of the video's they couldn't get a good look at the gentleman's face. Because he knows when to look and when not to look up which was very cleaver on his part. But one of the video's reveals his face while carrying Sheila on his shoulder. As exiting the seventh floor emergency stairwell which is a lot of stairs to go down. But the suspect with the victim took them and got away. But just as the family started to leave. The security team came to the Bentford's and ask Sam if he could come and identify a certain man in one of the video's that has Sheila over his shoulder. As walking a bit fast to the security room to verify to what's going on. Both Sam and Jon started shouting at security for letting this happen. "How in the heck you all let this man in here and he has my daughter?" ask sam.

"Mr. Bentford we didn't let this happen sir." said one of the officers. "But we would like for you to look at this video to see if you can reconized this guy in it." said one of the officers. "I look at the video several times and he looks a bit spooky like he is part animal then man." said the officer. "I never seen anything like this at all." said another officer. As trying to make out at what they are looking at was kinda confusing to them all why everyone just gaze at the screen.

But while looking at the video jon felt an adrenaline rush coming on as he kept glancing at the screen. "Yes I know that son of a bastard!" said Jon. "Yes sir we know him and he has my daughter sh--!" said Sam. "Well sir let us notify the sheriff offices if you all don't mind." said one of the officers. "Hey! You all can do whatsoever the f#*k you wants to do we are going to get my daughter back! Terra jonny let's go!" said Sam. "That muthaf#*ker!!!" said Sam in a very angry tone leaving the hospital. "That slow talking prick! He better not hurt her! that's all that matters!" said Sam. Now as leaving the hospital the sky lit up in lightening as a storm rolls through with heavy thunder and also rain. But that's not going to stop the Bentford's from getting the daughter and sister back in one peace.

"What in the heck man! Did you see that Jonny!?" "Dad i'am tryin to figure one thing at most and that is why do Ed has Sheila!? And what do he want with her!?" ask Jonny.

"I know one thing is that she better not be harm!" said sam. "That mutha—cker!! son of a -itch!" said sam. "Honey calm down don't let yourself get to work up." said Terra.

"Don't tell me to calm down! This is my baby girl we are talking about damn it!" said Sam. As Terra just gazed at Sam's whole demeanor. It's hard to see his behavior change just like that when it comes down to his children's the man means business. With his bad health sam needs to follow his girlfriend/ nurse sayings.Because Sam is very vulnerable to getting to sick easily without noticing his symptoms are on edge.

Before everything went down the Bentford's did notice that the locomotive has stop sitting in it usual spot right in back of the Bentford's home. Thinking maybe it change routs and move on or just waiting for the right time to strike. But with June's disappearance and now Sheila's abduction the men of the family are on point to kill at will if necessary to get back what is theirs. No it's and's about it kill on sight now that what's matter. The saying is that no man can be friends of the devil because satan is full of treacherously and deceitfulness. You can put your bottom dollar on any matter when it comes to him. In this matter Ed did make allegiance with Satan for power to destroyed his enemy. But Satan doesn't give a hootin nanny about no one but himself.

As Ed get set to go and do more damage to the family. He grabs his bestfriend ever that is his locomotive. As he steps up on his weapon of destruction to go and sit in back of his friend or foe's house to get him to come out. But sam and jon are on their way to his house to get Sheila back with loaded gun's and ready as ever to confront the enemy on it's grounds. In which can be also deadly if not careful.

But both father and son are ready for war as ever. The thing is trying to get to them in one peace like hell. But Sam do know and sense getting back his daughter isn't going to be easy and not even pretty. But when choosing war there are casualities for both sides. And it's ashamed that people chose to be a victim of death. Instead of doing the right thing and live a better life but though doing whatsoever right may still cost consequences. In today society people would rather be evil then meek and humble caring for one another and not so greedy and give more. But the tyranny is capitalism globalist socialism and mix with brutality. What a world we live in. Right?. And with hatred and racism still in existence that would've have been buried centuries ago.

But the earlier generations don't and want let thing be they would rather inbreeded it in their children's about violnce hatred and racism. Fingers are being pointed at the government for the mishap. Which controlling things that you may say. So really! who runs this giant crap of sin? A man! or many men! of a lousy system that failed us all. We all knows what a think tank is right? A group of people that sits around a table trying to cause mayhem in a once praying nation and now a modern day Sodom and Gomorrah you may say. But Babylon really is the name for this great and not so great of a place to be. Now arriving at Ed's place the Bentford's and Terra parks in front of the house in case Ed decides to come out and act like a sort of a nut case. But he house looks totally dark inside. But Ed's car is in the driveway it is still warm from running. "Why Terra I need for you to stay inside the truck." said Sam. "Jon you take the back door i'll take the front door." said Sam. While waiting inside the truck Terra started to feel a little sick. Not a cold sick but morning sickness. As she opens the door of the truck to regurgitate onto the ground like it's nobody darn business.

Sam was on the front porch of Ed's house. When he notice what Terra had done. "Hey you are you ok?" ask Sam. "I just feel so lousy for some reason." said Terra. "Hey dad, I don't see no one inside." said Jon. "Is she ok?" ask Jon.

"She said that she feels lousy." said Sam. "What in the heck did you eat Terra?" ask Sam. But Terra has a good sense to know whats going on as a female her body is going thru changes when she is about to experience motherhood.

In which she isn't ready for but what a suprise it would be to Jon becoming a father to Terra's baby. And a disgraces and disappointment on Mr. Bentford's behalf. Now that the family is going thru a rough period in their lives it just got much gritty. Now Sam doesn't suspect a thing but he will when he finds out that his beloved young girlfriend and his only loving son that he trust and love more then himself is more defile then a cat loving a dog on a bad day. It will eat Sam's insides up for to know that they commit fornication right under his nose. And now that in a few months to come baby bumps will appear and that's when questioning comes from Sam. And as Sam making a suggustion to stick around to see if they would come out of the house for any reason but still no sign of anyone is inside. "Shucks!

I still can't believe that Ed is a kidnapper." said Sam. "Tell me this what in God's name does he want with Sheila anyway?" ask Sam. "If anything ever happens to her he is definitly required a ass whooping for me alone." said Sam.

"How in the name of God can he remove my child from her hospital bed without my consent?" ask Sam. "Dad!

What are we going to do?" ask Jon. "By the way it's getting late." said Jon. Well Sam did what most fathers would do. "Well i'll kick his door in fuck it." said Sam. "The son of a bitch has my daughter!" said sam. Bang! Bang! The door opens. The house was dark inside not a move of anything. "Dad! Look they were here." that's Sheila's shoe ain't it?" ask jon. As Jon went to the other rooms of the house he notice that one room was lock with a padlock. But the other room was empty. But the one with the lock on the door had Jon thinking with curiosity wandering what was behind that door. Sam cover the kitchen and basement. Then some thing trigger their sense of smell. "Jonnie!" Sam calls. And Jon comes a running to see what his father wants. "Dad! Here I am." said Jon. "Do you smell that?" ask Sam. "Yeah it smells like a animal is in here with us and it smell like that thing we was fighting that night when it jumped out of the tree in the front yard." said Jon. "Why do I have a gut feeling that this creature and Ed are working together." said Sam. Shouldn't we make a call to sheriff Protzman's office?" ask Jon. "You can give him a call but we are going to handle this situation ourselves. If you don't mind." said Sam.

"Sorry dad I just think that this is getting really personal for us to handle alone you think?" ask Jon. As Sam grabs Jon by the shoulders. "Hey listen to me son!" "That psychopath of a friend of ours has my daughter your sister and all the sheriff is really going to do is send us home to wait a less six months to a year before we get a call from them." said Sam. "To tell us what we already know what a crock of bullshit!" said Sam. "So if this creature and Ed are working together? Well that means ed and that stanking son of a bitch of a monster its curtains for the both of them." said Sam. "Hey son check on Terra for me." said Sam. As Jon walks towards the truck. Terra's eyes have gotten bigger for to get Jon alone to break the news to him. "Hey Terra! Are you alright out there?" ask Jon. "Hey you I needs to speak to you for a moment and alone." said Terra.

"Ok what?" ask Jon. "Listen I missed my monthly cycle Jonnie." said Terra. "Sorry I don't follow you Terra." said Jon. "Damit man! I trying to tell you that i'am pregnant." said Terra. As Jonnie stood there with his mouth open and a bit of a shock for him. And it would be very devastating to the old man. As Jon acts like a typical guy would when he is in shock and scared. "How do I know it's mines?" ask Jon. "Look here you is the only guy I have gotten intimate with so don't play me Jon." said Terra. "Hold the –ck up!" said Jon. "So now! you just going to drop this on me like i'am a fool?" ask jon. "Hey man! I didn't tell you to lay with me." said terra. "But you might as well. shit!" said Jon.

"Look here! So you and my dad never had sex?" ask Jon.

"Now you know your father is very inpotent because of his meds." said Terra. "But i know how to settle this with a dna test when the baby arrive." said Terra. As Jon looks at her and calls her very pathetic as he walks away from her. "Sorry Jon! for this little suprise I have sprung on you like this I didnt mean any harm." said Terra. "Yes your ass did mean harm!" said Jon. As Jon walks back to the truck and ask Terra a important question. "I have one more question for you." said Jon. "How are we going to explained this situation to my father in what happen between us?" ask Jon. "Well your a big boy I was going to let you do that on your own." said Terra. "Well when i do explained this to him you better have your bags pack and ready to get out of lajunta." said Jon. "Because not only I betrayed him you also crossed him to but both of us is very wrong and defile for messing around behind his back." said Jon. Now as both side are trying to figure out how to tell the old man. But when he hear about this crazy nonsense it may shut him down mentally and physically. Timing has to be right when it comes to the old man. Sam can be a teddy bear at times and also a father that can't be taken for granted. "Jon!Come here!" Sam calls."You see this?" ask Sam. About the padlock on the door. "Oh yeah I saw it then I thought what is so important for him to keep a padlock on this door?" Jon's thought. "Again he has Sheila and all means are necessary!" said sam. "Dad I agree so let's kick it in." said Jon. "On three one two and three!" Both men kick as hard as ever.

Bang! Crunch! The door come open the room had a odour that was awfully stinch the place up. "Oh my Lord!" said Sam. "This is ridiculous! Who in their right mind lives like this?" ask Jon.

With a nasty disasted and filthy living wasn't Ed's way of living. But he was a single man that owns his own business without a wife and children to come home to a descent and in order household. "Dad look at this." said Jon. With a wall full of pictures of the bentford's home and Sam Jon and Sheila. Their every move they every done. "Whoa! Wait a darn minute this is what we are looking for. Wouldn't you know it." said Sam. "Ain't that Ed ass standing on that locomotive with the same color and upside down numbers?" that parks right behind the house? ask sam. "Yeap that's him." said Jon. "I hate to say it but it was Ed and this damn creature are working all together. And all the lone that man had something to do with the murders in this town." said Sam. "Where is he!!?" shouts Sam. "Good question." said Jon. In the meantime the locomotive that Sam and Jon had saw in the photo was ed's locomotive that did take the lives of other innocent victims that includes June sam's wife and son in law Jay Sheila's husband and several others.

But now the truth is sorted exposed but not to sure to say if Ed is connected to the creature but knows that Ed does have Sheila that he is caught on the hospital's camera carrying Sheila's helpless body out of the building. And Sam doesn't want the law involved in this situation. Sam wants to solved this one on it's own. "Look at this dad." said Jon. A photo of June in the backyard standing on the porch looking on over the corn field. And when Sam saw that photo of the love of his life he immediately started to get very emotional in which he misses his darlng wife of many years.

And now it's revenge time or let's say retaliate equals retribution for the family sake. It's a matter of time before the two men and a creature would dare to cross paths. And when that occurs it would be a fight of the century to where it would be talk about for years to come. The question is what lead up to the day of mayhem? And why are both men are having their differences solved this way?. Among others no one doesn't know why did Ed take Sheila from her room at the hospital it's a little perculiar for someone else to remove someone else family without permission. When it comes to the children's sake no one can win. Because the bible itself tells us what christ had said on offending a child that you mightest well hang a milestone from your neck and in the sea you go. A true and common fact that no one wants to hurt a child in no way at all. And in fact there is reprecussions when you mess with a man's daughther or mother's son and not expect a bit of words from the mouth.

Now that everything was exposed too. Sam's spirit was a good and wholesome until now. Sam and family are very prejudices against those who are trying to do harm then show mercy and love. So how is it that someone can show respect and no mercy or kindness and no love? Hate you and don't even know you?. But Sam had initiated this situation long ago by being Ed's friend and foe throughout schools years.

Sam made fun of Ed and talk badly behind his back when Ed meets a certain young lady sam would move in on Ed's girlfriends. And Sam would talk the girlfriends into being with his instead. And the young ladies was in love with Sammy the ladies man. That was sam's nickname throughout his school years. But Sam did show a little anger when someone did call him sammy he didn't not know. "It's Sam to you." said Sam. To Ed it was special Ed cause of the classes he took were special classes for under achievement more like learning development. So that's why ed never gotten alone in school period. Ed tried his best to make friends but it always leads into a disagreement some how. With him wants to fight. Ed always had a anger problem to where he didn't get alone with others. Even when he was just a toddler. Ed would bite scatch and pull hair. Ed was a hand full and a piece of work. But being the only child Ed was very spoiled and highly favor in his parents eyes. But others would say different cause others have seen a different side of Ed. Ed can be a descent student if he wanted to. But when you have other students coming to bother you for no reason and constantly nagging and picking what else can you do to defend yourself?. The one to come and pick would be no other then Sam himself. All throughout grade school Sam would pick and nagged his so called best buddy in which got Ed into trouble most of the time. But Ed didn't care to get into trouble all he wanted was June to be his girlfriend.

But Sam step in the way of that relationship by keeping Ed into trouble Sam could lured June into his corner and Ed is without a girlfriend for the fifth time. Because of Sam's tactics. "Oh boy what a friendship". See every girl that Ed befriended some how Sam would run a interference and cost Ed the relationship. So Ed had all this bottled up inside from years of hurt and not having the guts to tell Sam how he really feel about his friendship. Now the time is close for both men to cross paths just like a thunder storm is about to take place over all of Lajunta. As it would for citizens run for cover getting out of the way of the heavy down pours and thunder with lightening so violent that everyone sits still and looking for terrified.

Always About You

Chpt XIV

Now still on the trail of Ed and Sheila's and trying to know their whereabouts are like looking for a needle in a barn of straw. And Ed and with Sheila as his hostage tied up sitting on the floor of the engine shaken and cold. In Sheila's confused mind hope that her family would find her before it's to late. Having a psychopath in her presence was scarey enough to someone who was well known to the family but is a true and vicious monster. But sometime the person that held you when you were a infant to a toddler is a dangerous mind could harm the heart. Now that ed is waiting on Sam to appear at the back door of his home so he can make a even swop the daughter for Sam. "Where in the hell is your freakin father?! "I'am running low on patients my sweet and beautiful girl!!" said Ed.

With Ed still in human form but both of his eyes are in a red and blue colors that would spook anyone that dares to stare. With his fingers starting to grow long then the talons would come next. And as the creature state would take over Ed's body there no turning back until the spell wears off.

Suddenly a light comes on in the kitchen at Sam place to cause Ed's transfiguration to slow down because in a creatture's state it's hard for Ed to communicate as a creature. As the rev of the engine and sound the horn to get sam and Jon to come out to see him before killing Sheila. But sounds of horns again then the lights went out and the back door came open. With both men and Terra at their side. As everyone had a weapon loaded and ready to killed with all means necessary. "Terra you stay near the house while Jon and i put a bullett in this muthf***er head." said Sam. With Sam and Jon both yelling for Ed to come off the locomotive and face them like a man with guts or with a creature with him. "Ed!

You son of a bitch! C'mon! so we can fix this thing between us!" said Sam. "We know what you are all about!" said Jon.

"We know you are a cowarded of a man hiding behind a filthy stanken and worthless creature!" said Sam. The engine was running but no signs of Ed and Sheila on board. So both Sam and Jon walk towards the engine slowly with a eye for cautions. So the men split up by surrounding the engine. "Shucks!" said Sam. "This is the wrong engine!" said Sam. "What the f**k!!" said Jon. A older gentleman heard both Sam and Jon talking near the engine so he came out to see what was all the comotion near the tracks. "May I help you guys?" ask the engineer. "Sorry sir! We thought you was somebody else!" said Sam. "Well who is it you looking for?" ask the engineer. "A man by the name of Edward Dart." said Sam. "Never heard of him." said the engineer. "He ride a locomotive just like you." said Sam.

"Mister I know everyone that works for the company and there isn't a Edward Dart that works for the company.

"But I do know this that one of our locomotive's has being missing for a while and no one has seen it." said the engineer. "Hey wait a minute I have a photo with him in it you don't recognize this fellow?" ask Sam. "Sorry to say I don't know him sir and what did he do if you don't mind me asking?" ask the engineer. "This guy has my daughther! And he use to be a friend of the family!" said Sam. "Now he's a stone cold enemy to us!" said Jon. As the gentleman return to the cab of the locomotive to leave he watch Jon and Sam returned to the back of the house with rifles in their hands.

Now the waiting game is in tact to see if that train will show up eventually. But that same locomotive is in the next two countys. With Sheila lying on the floor of the locomtive with nothing on but a hospital gown. Ed is starting to act a little naughty by gazing up and down Sheila's body while she lays helpless on the warm side of the cab. Ed mind was boggling about messing with his former friend daughter would really stir the pot of war between the two.

But Ed wanted a taste and feel of a females anatomy. Because the truth is that Ed hasn't had a woman in years. Not a lone having any sex with a female so with that said the man is out of his mind and blaming sam for the way things are. As in the middle of nowhere Ed started to feel a little horny as he grabs himself with one hand and place other hand on Sheila's thigh and hip as he turned her over on her back to get a great view of her just laying there before he can put the pieces together. "Not bad at all for to be so young as you are." said Ed In a rusty tone. As he starts to act really wearied by sticking himself to Sheila's body. But Sheila it felt even wearied to her for her to start fighting him off of her. "If you don't keep your damn hands off of me i'll kill you myself!!" said Sheila. "You freaking pervert!!" said Sheila. "I was trying to see if you was ok." said Ed. "But do you have to touch me!! said Sheila. As Ed get a little upset over the name calling and then he grabs Sheila by her hair and said "Watch your tone young lady i'll tell you what to do alright!!" said Ed. "And you heard what I said too damit!" said Sheila. "I don't understand men the way you all act towards females period!" said Sheila. "Like what!?" ask Ed. "Why do you men always think that a woman always have sex on the brain?" ask Sheila. "Well all men are different when it come to that." said Ed. "And yes I do love women with all do respect but I know that some of you women are a little crazy at times. "And your not!?" asked Sheila. "You got neves to call somebody crazy!" said Sheila.

"But i'am going to tell you a story about your old man and I you asked why is this happening? Well your mother was my girlfriend at first until your daddy brought his no good ass into your mother and I business." said Ed. "He also got into her head then she end up with his sorry ass!" said Ed.

"So I had to take your mother out of the equation to get to him."said Ed. "You son of a bitch! You killed my mom!?

Oh just wait you will get yours!!" said Sheila. "So killing her because she didn't want to be with you asshole so what did it prove?! That you are a stone cold killer!!" said Sheila.

"It proved that your father didn't deserve her and I was tired of hearing all the good stuff that he was doing." said Ed. "When you untied me I will tried to kill you myself!" said Sheila. "You bitch! I told you to watch your tone and how you speak to me damit!!" said Ed. "So you keep on talking the way you doing I will put you also with your dead mother!" said Ed. "Would you like to joined her? huh!" ask Ed. "I can make it happen!" said Ed. As Sheila quiets down and sat with a deadly stare on her face hoping that she can found a way to get a loose from this evil person. In the book of James 3:16 tells the story. For where envying and strife is there is confusion and every evil work.

Therefore with everything exposed Ed would need to unleash that monster that's inside him soon Because he can't take on the Bentford's by himself he would get a beating for life without that entity within. Because he knows for sure that Sam and son would be to much to handle. But with the creature's involvement would it be as well to much for Sam son and weapons?. But the creature has attributes to uses for his advantage. Like make himself invisible to camouflage himself to blend in for the surroundings. His height is seven feet tall with talons on hands and feet. And not to forget the scent that is so undepicable that makes the air hard to breath in. So Ed has the upper hand in dominance the Bentford's has the upper hand in weapons at their disposal.

As the night turns colder both men are winding down from a week of misery and heartaches from Sheila's whereabouts.

The main concern is that she is still alive but what kind of condition is she in? With it being as cold as it is she would freeze to death. With Sam and Jon thinking that Ed has a killing coming to him. He just went completely over board with this petty kidnappng he has going on. Which is very lame of him to get someones attention by taking something off of the porch or maybe throw eggs at the house or let's toilet paper the whole yard. But taking someones child is a little bit of extreme. As both men walks into the house to get ready to take a shower and grab a beer with a bite to eat. But Sam sat next to Terra on the sofa to take a load off of his feet trying to make up sometime with her. "Baby with all that is going on I apologized to you for this mess that I had to exposed for you to see." said Sam. "O' honey you don't have to apologize." said Terra. "Well I thought that I should do so still." said Sam.

As Jon comes into the kitchen from outside he gave Terra the dirtiest look he can give her from their recent talk they had earlier in the week. But Jon knows that his father is going to know sooner or later when Terra starts to show. It not so obvious for a woman try to hide her pregnancy to the one that matter most to her. But when something is wrong she tried to stay to herself and shut everyone out that maybe against her. "After all that is going on I have to tell you something in a serious matter." said Terra. "Well tell me now or I will find out sooner or later." said Sam. So as Terra starts to tell Sam what she wants him to know about her and Jon the phone ringing. Hoping that it would be news about Sheila's whereabouts. "Hello!" said Sam.

It's the law on the other end. "Sam!" this is Sheriff Protzman's office." we may have a lead on where your daughther may be at this moment. But not quite sure yet." said the officer.

"So stay near the phone sir and we will keep in touch to give you updates about the case sir." said the officer. "i will call you back as well." said Sam. "Hey Jonnie! That was the sheriff's office they said that they may have a lead on your sister's whereabouts but not quite sure." said Sam. "With the sheriff department looking for my daughther I don't believe it." said Sam. "What do you don't believe?" ask Terra.

"Well they couldn't get a lead on my wife's whereabouts! So what makes Sheila's case such of a easy lead?" ask Sam.

"Well maybe it's something the sheriff office may see now that they didn't see before." said Terra. "Sam honey. Don't get all work up over the situation let the authority handle the case. Please!" said Terra. "You are right sweetheart that is why I love you." said Sam. In a instantaneously Terra's smile left her face in a frown mode when Sam told her those loving words that every woman loves to hear. But not this time because those same words will leave sam in a state of a shock and hurt. While Jon is in thee other room eavsedropping on his father's conversation with Terra. But he heard his father tell Terra that he love her but didn't hear Terra's reply back. As Jon wonder if Terra had told his the truth of what happens when he is sleeping. While Terra gets up to go to the bathroom she stops in Jon's bedroom to ask questions. "Jon how are we going to tell him about what happen between us?" ask Terra. "I don't know Man! I knew I shouldn't mess around with you." said Jon.

But you like it and you wasn't saying anything when you was getting it now was you?" ask Terra. "Look here you f**king heifer! you came at me and initiated the situation." i'am here for good and not going anywhere I need a father for the baby sake so live it and love it get use to it." said Terra. As Jon sat there with a mean and bitter look that could kill with an instant. "If I didn't know any better I think you did it to trap me." said Jon. "Maybe I didn't maybe I did but oh well it happen." said Terra. "And you like it too." said Terra. "Ughhhh!" said Jon. "You bitch!" said Jon immediately Jon grab some clothes and a few other items to run out of the house for a getaway before he can murder a woman or he get murder by his father for messing around with his father's companion. But Jon knows that he must face his father soon or later. Before it's to late. Now as Jon stops in his tracks knowningly he cant leave his father unattentend and knows that creature is out there with Ed. So Jon is thinking about telling his father everything that went on with him and Terra behind his back.

But it's not going be easy doing so after he said what he said about messing with Terra but she came messing with Jon. But Jon known better to go against his father's wishes.

Jon is a strong young man but he let a beautiful girl come between him and his father like it's no one business.

And now Jon has to let his father know about such things as having to fornicate in his home with the girl his dad fell in love with. But its not all of Jon's fault alone. But he did let it happen. Jon could've prevent things from going to far again he did allowed a girl come between him and his dad.

As things may get rough between Sam and Terra but father and son it should remained the same as of now. But Jon wishes Terra would go on and tell his father the truth about them both. And what happen between them both. But that is what men do by allowed the woman become the main culprit men are not friends anymore. Therefore the bible is absolutely true when lust overcomes a man's heart. Some how he becomes blind from his own sin. The woman is the fruit in which she becomes more pleasant to the human eye of the man. The more he looks at her the more the looks becomes sweeter until it feels good to him and her. Then the exposure from her follows then. Just as a baby sees a bottle of milk once the infant has it in it's mouth then it quiet down.

Well Jon had a taste of the sweet feeling of sex many times over with Terra and now the consequences alone with the reprecussions for disobedient towards his father's rule. Just arrived in amount of minutes. Jon figures he doesn't have anything to loose but his father's trust and a friend. Now Jon is thinking it would be great to tell his father the truth right about now. "Hey dad can I see you for a moment?" ask Jon. "why sure son." said Sam. "What is it son?" ask Sam. As Jon tense up going over to the kitchen table to have a seat next to his father. Trying to find the words to say in a plain and simple way. "Dad I have something to confessed up about and whatever you do to me I probably deserve it."said Jon."Well son what are you talking about?

You are scaring me." said Sam. "Terra and I have been sleeping with each other." said Jon. After Jon made a tempt in telling his old man the truth a surprisng knock was at the door. It was the sheriff department with some undoubtful news about Sheila was she at peace with her mother or they found her rape and beaten by Ed.It could be a string of things that could be told. As Sam started to speak on the situation he heard it again the knock at the door. While Jon hurried to the door to see who it was. It was the deputies from the sheriff department that needed to talk to Sam &

Jon on Sheila's last time of being seen and what lead up to her disappearance. But Sam as with Jon also knew not to say anything about the creature and what they want to do themselves. They kept it quieted and not say a word of the strategy that's in mind. Sam play non chalant about what was said at the hospital. Because one of the deputies heard Sam and Jon both comments on carrying out threats against another individual. Who?

During the hospital visit to see Sheila but the staff and the hospital security team over heard father & son threating to killed dart for removing Sheila from her hospital room. So many over heard the two using verbal threats of killing someone but didnt know who they were talking about. Unto they were talking about the individual that's in the monitor removing their family member.

"Hi Mr. Bentford we have a few questions to ask you& Jon both." said one deputy. "Go ahead we are listening" said Sam. "On the night at the hospital when you both were shown the individual that removed your daughther from her room did you both knew that individual?" ask one of the deputies. And as Sam looks at his son and Jon did the same to think of something quick to say before speaking in other words lying to the authorities. "Yes & No." said Sam. "I said yes I do know him but no I didn't think he was capable of pulling something like he did." said Sam.

"So you all know him?" ask the one deputy. "Yeap!" said Sam. "My question is have y'all seen my daughther?" ask Sam. "Mr. Bentford we are trying our hardest to find your daughther's whereabouts sir." said the deputy. "Well! the freakin problem is for y'all to come here to ask my son and I questions!?" and not found my daughther?" ask Sam.

"Oh boy! Yall got some kinda nerves to come here to put us on freakin trial!" "Wow! said Sam."Far as I'am concerned this interrogation is over until you guys bring my daugther back to me!." "But I have one more question for you." said the deputy. "No! Goodnight officers!" said Sam. Now that the officers are leaving here come the thunder from Sam. "Now son explained to me what you said before the deputies arrived." said Sam. "About Terra and I have being sleeping with each other for a moment." said Jon. "What the f—k!! are you talking about boy!!?" ask Sam. "Dad! i'am here to confess my guilt because Terra and I can't look you in the eyes and say we love you and going behind your back to see one another it's not fair dad to you." said Jon.

"We both are tired of hiding this ridiculous fornication." said Jon. Now while everything was going on and well said in the kitchen among father and son Terra was trying to remove herself from thee equation by packing her belongings and leaving. But she notice that all of suddenly it got real quiet in the kitchen so she stop packing to go and see what was going on in the other part of the house. When Terra got to the kitchen the back door was wide open with both Jon and Sam outside pushing one another around and cursing and at each other.

Until one point Jon pushed his old man down to the ground and sat on him as Sam laid there full of anger for what his dear and beloved son has done. Now with Terra standing and looking on and crying at what she had created also. By coming between a father and son. But in everyway not cool at all. And if Sheila was presence it would have being a double fight. But Terra knows better to come between a family and not receive a blow for a punishment also. Now that the truth and everyone's secrets are being revealed there is one more thing that needs to be exposed also. Terra's pregnancy will cause sam's much heartaches and pain and adding miserey knowing he would be grandfather to his girlfriend's child. It's just wasn't right at all in Sam's sight.

So sam is going to do something in which he hate doing and that is putting both Jon and Terra out of his house. Jon finally let his father up off the ground with Sam standing up and angry as heck cursing both Jon and Terra for what they did. "Sam! I'am so sorry!" said Terra. "Actully! Dad we both are sorry!" said Jon. "I want both of you! Out!!" said Sam. "Dad wait you don't mean that really?" ask Jon. "Get the hell out!!" said Sam. With his loud behavior with his back towards them. Sam wouldn't even look at them. Because he was absolutely hurt bad by his young girlfriend and beloved son. He felt so betrayed people he well love and trust with everything he every had. Life and the world is just so funny like that sometimes. But the ones that are hurt are the ones that are needed the most in the long run.

You can put your bottom dollar on this situation and still comb it with a fine tooth. But before the week is out sam will missed both Jon and Terra just like they misses Sheila. Sam knows being alone in the house really comprimised him and make him so vulnerable like a sitting duck during hunt season. Wishing that his wife was with him right now as he sat at his kitchen table wepting and totally hurt. First his wife then his daughter kidnapping by his so call bestfriend now the son gets his young girlfriend pregnant and not to mention there's a creature that trying to kill him and his family. How much more can this elder gentleman of this well kept community take? Sam is a strong man who stood his grounds and kept his family from all harm hurt and danger. But come to him who would protected Sam? Now it's getting close for paths to crossed.

When the bible speaks on Armageddon what come to mind?

Well a place where good and evil will battle one another for the final conflict. People will live and also people will die.

Shall evil live? Or shall good die off? Whatsoever will happens Sam house will eventually become the battle ground.

Now that Jon and Terra had left the house leaving Sam at a terrible time and well messed up in the head. Sam had consider taking his life after all that transpired in a short amount of time. But Sam must remained focus if he is planning to get his daughther back in one peace. And beat the crap out of Edward Dart or battle a creature that wants him and the rest of his family dead. Believe it or not. Sam has a lot of tricks up his sleeves. But the right time and day to use it on the creature and ed. But reality will sat in when Sam or maybe Jon will figure out who's who in this situation before everything align up as havoc boils over. Just like getting ready for a game where everyone is so geek up and excited.

But things must take place before seeing Sheila again and Jon return home and settle things wth his father. And Terra has to get Sam to accept her for her faults. Because Sam is going to step out in faith and handle Ed himself. A weird knock at the front door distracted Sam's thinking about what had happen between him and his son. Sam went and grab his weapon before going to see who is at the door and it's Terra for some reason she returned to talk Sam into letting her come back for a little while. But Sam thought it was so weird for her to returned without Jon. So he had mercy on her and let her in. But the real unusual thing was the look she gave Sam when she walk through the door. Like she was going to do damage to this older gentleman she once love. "Terra what's wrong and where's is my son and why are you cover in blood!?" ask Sam. As Terra just stood there looking at Sam with a evil look. Then and there Sam knew something was wrong deep down in his heart that Terra did a evil play on his son. Sam grabs Terra and started to shake some sense into her. "Terra what happen!?" ask Sam. As she started to speak her words came out as mambo jambo why Sam was trying to understand her but very little she said Sam just couldn't quite understand her still. "Terra!

Again I'm asking you where is Jon!?" ask Sam. Then she walk over towards the sofa and collapse between the sofa and coffee table.

Sam not realizing that Terra has a knife in her left hand as Sam trying to lift her onto the sofa as he examine her as she laid there cover in blood Sam noticed the knife in her left hand but she wasn't bleeding. So this is someone else's blood. Thought Sam. As Sam has a terrified look and worried that Terra did something wrong to his son. Sam walks to the kitchen to dial the paramedic's and explained to them that there's a young lady needs some medical attention. Then he hang the phone up. As he turned around to go back to the livingroom Terra was standing there with that knife in her left hand looking at Sam with a evil look walking towards him. Saying stuff that Sam couldn't believe he is hearing this with his own ears. "Well Sam I think I kill you next like I killed your son!" said Terra."Wait a minute damn you!" said Sam."Terra! Why are you doing this!?"ask Sam.

"I was sent by my father to keep an eye on you and your stupid son." said Terra. "Excuse me!! who is your father if i may ask!?" ask Sam. "Enough! Talking!" said Terra. As Terra started to take swings at Sam she cuts his right arm to get him to fight her. "So all this was a setup to come into my home to killed us? In other words you never care about me and my family did you?" ask Sam. "But again who is your father?" ask Sam."That man that has your daughter is my father!" said Terra. "What in the hell!" said Sam."That is so right! And where you are going!" said Terra. As Terra chase Sam around the sofa into the kitchen around the kitchen table hoping that someone would show up and give him a hand in handling Terra crazy butt.

But Sam would have to make it right with Jon if he shows up. Terra is starting to get a lot aggressive being in a neutral way. "Look Terra we can talk about it i'll give you what ever you want." said Sam. "I don't need anything from you at all but one thing!" said Terra. "what is that I may ask?" ask Sam."your life!!" said Terra. Sam spotted a frying pan that was in the sink and nail Terra upside her head as hard as he could to put her out like a light enough time to tie her hand behind her. Sam thinking that Jon is alright. But must go and find him and quick. Because time is running out for him and his kids. As Sam thought it would be wise to call the authorities and report a break in at his place and then leave. So they can pick up Terra crazy butt. As Sam was leaving the phone rang the sheriff office was calling to let Sam know that they found Jon on the hotel floor left for dead but he is going to make it. Where a housekeeper found him and reported it. Terra stab Jon in his left arm when Jon slapped her for talking bad about his parent's and told her if she do it again that he would kill her. But Terra beat him to the punch by using a knife from room service.

As Jon turns his back for a moment then Terra had it her way by knocking Jon down on the bed and went to work on him. As Jon lays helpless on the floor of their hotel room then Terra went to call her father then let him know what she had done. Ed gave is daughther credit for that evil deed she had done." Daddy! I think I killed this no good son of a bitch." said Terra. "where's the bitch at or do you still have her?" ask Terra. "I'm thinking about cutting her head off and throwing it in the river." said Ed. "I need for you to go back to the house and try to get her old man." said Ed."Babygirl finish it for me."said Ed.

Therefore she did as her father command her to do. What a way for evil to spread itself as fast as good can happen.

But no evil deeds can go unpunished or say unreconized.

As everything starts slightly to align itself according to Ed's plans with the help of a daughter out of wedlock with a hooker he met outside of his auto part's store. Her name was Terri Comers she was absolutely wild and didn't care about anything but herself and money. Terri loves to get high in back of Ed's store until he caught her and another girl in back of his store so stone they both didn't know which way was home. But when Ed took out the trash for the evening before closing up he busted them sitting on his property and getting high as a kite.So Ed grabs Terri arm and the other girl ran but he made sure that he grabs the right one. Ed had his eyes on Terri for awhile. And now what a sweet moment for him to get her. See Terri was a gorgeous gal.That every guy talks about Terri and what they did for a one night stand it all over the town. But Terri didn't mind any of the publicity for her it was a way to be self employed. And make big bucks at it.

So Ed kept Terri hostage until he call on the authorities to pick her up. But instead of the authorities showing up Terri had other things in mind for Ed. As spending time in the back of his shop with a young woman who made Ed feel like a man should. Ed did allowed Terri to go where no female lips ever went before until now. Terri had made Ed so horney he picks her up and moved everything that was on his desk to the floor to lay Terri on her back and they both got naked. When Ed saw Terri naked his testosterones went nuts and other words very excited to lay with her. It was his first and last time he would make love with a female.

One day at Ed's shop it was extremely busy three months had come for Terri to march into Ed's shop to tell him bold news in front of his employees that she is pregnant. But Ed act like he didn't know what she was talking about. Ed took her by her hand and lead her to his office so they can discussed their affairs privately. Because a woman doesn't like being ignored when it comes to getting her point across to whom ever. As well as men doesn't like being embarrased in front of others. As people often say whatsoever it pleases them. But words are known to hurt others.

Because people only say what's in their heart. So Ed and Terri started shouting with much profanity was used like crazy you would think that you were at a boot camp or a military school listening to a couple of drill captains going at it. As customers and employees alike just stood still and listen to every word that was said and used. Now both Ed and Terri's business is out to dry with the whole community knows from inviting Terri to his office to the moment they both had sex on top of his desk. But you see that no one can be discreet about their own affairs. What makes a bit of difference when they can uncover the other person business? When it's time to do damage to another. Society just wants to get even with a little of retribution which in make things feel good within. But in reality we all loose too.

Being igonorance is unfruitful to bite like crow is a tougher bird to eat and life itself is tougher then all.

A Hateful Surprise

Chpt XV

Therefore Ed and Terri needed some thoughts on how they going to raise a baby they didn't planned for but that how life sugar coated this situation. Both Ed and Terri knew that laying down together sounds real good to a man especially like Ed who is a womanizer and a well known perverted individual who didn't mind talking and undressing a woman the minute he lay eyes on. Ed lays in bed fantasizng about June all the time. Just hoping that him and her could be a couple for a day or two. And what he could've done for her and his children by her. And what her life could've been. But we can't never pick our family like your mind can pick up a fantasy in a drop of a hat why sure we can't be like christ have done to choose his family and hold the universe all together. A mind is terrible to hold decietfulness when it is feeding the heart also. With the mind set that Ed has to get rid of Terri and the baby was dangerous but differcult to do. Because she was with child. But after the birth Ed is determine to have June for the lady in his life simple as that and nothing wasn't getting in his way. But Terri and her unborn child. So eliminating them both would be necessary.

But Ed thought that waiting afterward's for Terri to have the baby then exposed himself to her then the killing would be necessary to do. Then the child would be without a mother and Ed would put the child up for an adoption or find a descent home for it. But we know that things never go as planned as always. By doing evil is so essential for Edward Dart. Now Terri was getting prepared to drop this baby in another six months with making Ed's life a living hell with cravings for certain foods and pains everytime she move on swollen feet and legs. But Ed thought it would be a good ideal to taken her and throw her off a cliff with the child inside of her but he backs off. Because he wants to see what this child would look like. Ed thought many times over if it's a boy he would welcome it with open arms but a girl he would have to think about that also having a girl

Ed would have to protected the child from himself when he is upset with things not going his way. Ed knows no one needs to see the other side of him. Therefore six months has come and gone;with Terri having the baby and everyone around the baby was sanctifyng how beautiful the baby was looking. As looking closely she can resemble both Ed and Terri with a head full of hair and also her big rosey cheeks she have. Surprising Ed shows up when the doctors had to induced labor. Because Terri's health wasn't the greatest for her to have a child. But also there was concerns about the baby's health also. Terri did drugs most of her life. This is a red flag for the doctor to look into this situation will not be tolerated. Children's services will be notify at once. As the doctors were talking to see if the father would raised the child himself but Ed stays to busy with the shop and his other pride and joy is that locomotive of his with a little bit of committing homicide's of course on the side.

Meanwhile Terri was stuck in the hospital on the doctor orders for a thorough evaluation before she could leave the hospital with the new born infant. But Ed was notify of the situation that Terri is a drug user. The test came back that the baby's system is also defected from Terri's uses of drugs.

But Ed is aware of this from the time he ran up on her and the girl. "It's sickening to here of this." said Ed. "So are you going to take the baby and take care of it?" ask the doctor.

"I suppose I can take care of her until the mother get herself together." said Ed.

As Ed had thought deeply of taken the baby and putting it in foster care from himself and it would be better for the baby's sake. Because Ed truly doesn't have the patiences for any children. And not to mention the otherside of evil that Ed has posessed over a woman that he truly love and had no intention of destroying her but letting his evil side get the best of him to demised others. But all these years have gone by but Ed never mention of having any kids at all. So with testing the childs health was not normal and Terri's is showing a mass over her lungs from smoking at a young age of thirteen. So the doctor had gather all of Terri's charts to give her all the bad news that no one wouldn't like to hear about taken the child away from it's mother. And there is a possibilitiy that Terri may not see her daughther grow up or hear and see her first walking steps. Terri named her after her. The baby name is Terra Dart. But McKenzie is her adopted last name to concealed who she really is.

Now that Terri's health is fast deteriorating from having lung cancer. She was told that she may have approximately six months to live. In Ed's mind he doesn't have to worry about taken Terri's life anymore. Because natural causes would do the trick for him. Ed did as he thought of putting the baby up for adoption. And Terri did succumbed to her cancer. Therefore Ed had no intentions to stay with Terri of course. June was still the apple in his eyes. But with June in a marriage to Sam that was playing with fire or maybe let's say Russian Roulette. But Ed didn't care he envy Sam's life for taking June away from him. And haven't gotten over it yet. Believe it or not Sam will hurt or kill anyone or someone over his family. But one neat thing that Ed did do was pay for Terri's creamation. Because Terri was also a child that was apart of the system in foster homes in and out of jail. And youth homes as well. But the only child without a family. But we all go through somethings regardless! We need God for a better world a better future. God is the only someone to confined in and not your average person. So God is the one to hear your call he's is the one that put you in bondage the one that can bring you out.

Furthermore God is so awesome in glory. A person like Ed who puts his trust in his evil side instead. With a mind like Ed's fill with evil and killings and envying is part of his nature. Like many years before getting a young woman like Terri pregnant with his seed. But his kid found him and now she a part of his life rather Ed like it's or not. Terra is helping her father destroyed the people who cause him so much hurt and pain in the previous years. But Terra doesn't know everything about her father's dark side of things but she is in for a rude awaking.

Back at the Bentford's residences Sam is thinking about his kid's well being. Hoping he would find them both before time runs out. As he stands in his kitchen looking down at Terra thinking where in the hell did she come from really.

Therefore Terra had to play and goes alone with her daddy's plans to get Sam Bentford and his family. If Ed and his daughter could just get Sam alone for the creature to finished him that is all that Ed would like but it want be easy with Jon still alive.

Now as Sam takes a seat at the kitchen table thinking where to start looking for Jon or Sheila whereabouts. As he thinks there is a ring from the phone it's the hospital calling on Jon's behalf letting Sam know that Jon is there trying to recover from a stab womb from Terra. "Hello!" Sam said. "Jon is this you?" Sam ask. "Mr. Bentford this is Lajunta Mermorial

Hospital we are calling to let you know that your son Jon Bentford is here and he is trying to recouperate from a stab womb in his left arm in which he lost a little bit of blood but he going to make after all."nurse said. Now that was a load off of Sam's shoulders. Great news for to move on for Sheila's whereabouts. Sam reaches down to pickup Terra and sat her in the chair across from him so when she does come to he got questions for her to answer too. "Terra! Or is that your real name!?"Sam ask. "Today is a day for me to seriously hurt someone or kill somebody!"Sam said.

As Terra started to come conscious out of the blow upside her head from a skillet she realized that she was tide up with her hands in the back of her so no crazy ideals that can happen. "Hey girl wake your ass up!."said Sam. As she come to she had a deadly stare in her eyes that couldn't be explained but Sam put everything together and he comes up with Terra and Ed are working together on doing damaged to him and his family for whatever reason Sam will never know."Why are you doing this!" "is it for money!? Sam ask.

"No! It's better then money!" Terra said. "It's you Sam that we want! You don't know what you did to my dad forty-three years earlier!" do you?" Terra ask. As Sam takes a closer look at Terra's eyes started to change colors as she talks about revenge and eliminating Sam and his family like her father already gotten June Jay and maybe Sheila and others that lives were casualties to her fathers destrution.

Some how all that Ed or the creature had killed those lives had a conflict with Ed in the past. In particular like the Chambers twins was murder for throwing gravel and being nosey in Ed's business. So they had to be rid of. June on the other hand wouldn't give herself to Ed. So to Ed if he can't have her no one else can have her neither. So she had to go as well. Ed's biggest project is to get rid of Sam especially then the children if necessary by all means. But as long as Sam's children are in the picture Ed and Terra can't seem to get the job done. "What in the hell did I supposedly do to your damn father!?" Sam ask. "You should know what you did!" Terra said. "Well let me tell you a little story about your no good father!." Sam said. "Ed and June were going together for a hot minute until she saw me and then it was all over for your damn father." "hahahaha!" Sam laughing.

"Well you can laugh all you want but we will have the last laugh!" You old son of b—ch!!" Terra said. "So was you really pregnant!? Or was that a lie to get my son by himself so you can harm him!?" Sam ask. "Let's say your boy isn't as smart as he looks!" Terra said. "You think I will let someone like you or him to inpregnant me!?" "No way in hell!"

Terra said. "I really like you! A lot!"said Sam. "As of now you ain't nothing but a little whore to me!"said Sam. "So that makes your daughter one! Right!?" Terra ask. "My kids is way better then you will ever be!" Sam said. "We will definitely see!" said Terra. "Yes we will!" said Sam.As Terra sat there in a chair across from the man that she called herself loving is her enemy. As she looks and stares at Sam with a vicious look but a deadly smirk on her face.

So Sam had an ideal that came off the top of his head is his daughter for a daughter. This is Sam's boldness and smart move he could think of to reason with Ed and the evil side And also for everyone not to get hurt or lives taken in the process.

Therefore Sam already knew that he couldn't trust Terra as far as he can throw her. So Sam left her tide up until he can get this figured out on what to do. "Sam! I got to pee!" said Terra. "i can drag your ass to the back porch and you can pee there!" Sam said. "Cmon! Sammy! I thought you said you love me!" said Terra. "Bit--! Shut the hell up!" said Sam. "if I get a loose you better begged for mercy!"

Terra said. "If you come a loose I swear on my wife's grave I will shoot you! So try me!!" Sam said. As Sam takes his.357 revolver out of the kitchens counter top draw. And place it on the table in front of Terra to make a serious statement that he will shoot her if she get a loose. "That gun doesn't scare me!" said Terra. "Well sweetheart it's not supposed to scare you! It's going to put a bullet in you for me!

Anymore smart remarks?"ask Sam. Now Terra holds her peace and not say another word. As Sam goes around to check Terra's restraints to make sure she doesn't try to escape from him. Now the evening was getting late with both men has each others daughter for a hostage. But Ed is going to his darkside of thing to come and see his old an best of friends. But before going Ed needs to contact his daughter to see whats up on his commands he has given to her in the early part of the week. To kill Bentford and his son. But she failed to comply with her fathers commands. So Ed has no way to get in touch with his daughter so he takes the conspicuous way of doing things by taking the locomotive by Sam's house with Sheila still alive and under dress.

But Sheila holds her grounds with Ed trying to seduce her at times but Sheila held him off of her. But if Ed was smart he would drive by Sam's to see if anyone was there. So he's looking for a fight instead that's what evil does. To start a mountain of trouble and drag as many people into it. Just like a war of a country that wants democracy or independency so war is thee answer for some people and others just be innocent victims and more casualties. But wasted lives for wanting peace and prosperity. Sam is waiting on Jon's release from the hospital for a helping hand to find Sheila.

But little that Sam knows that Ed is coming to him to kill Sheila right in front of him at the tracks. And Ed doesn't know much either that Sam is going to put a bullet into his daughter if Ed don't cooperate with his terms. So innocent girls has to died Because both men are at war with each other. Sam can't wait to wrap his hands around Ed's neck and stomp his face into the ground for the death of June and his son-in law Jay. But Sam has to realize that he isn't going up against Ed alone. The creature will be at hand and Jon is needed to be at hand as well. With Sam and Jon both can win this war against this creature with powers to make itself invisible and strenght of five to ten men. The height of a center on a basketball team and talons like a eagle. The bad part is it smells horrible out of human flesh. As time is approaching for the men to meet with each others daughter with Sam and Ed looking very optimistic about holding each others daughter for a hostage will be very interesting.

Now as Sam sits and watch Terra trying to get out of the restraints that he put her in. While she used so much profanity in calling Sam names. But Sam kept his cool as he just stares at Terra thinking how she had them all fooled into thinking that she was a great person to be around. Be that it told Sam seen a big butt and a smile and was hook into this sassy young and beautiful girl that was too young to handle. Now Sam must owed his kid's apology for bring danger into their habitation of love for each other.

The Bentford's home is base on love for each other not a day goes by that they don't show that they are a tight knitted family. If the parents show love and affection towards each other that the offsprings will be the same way. So that no one can come between anyone of them. But just this one time that Sam had let his guards down for a young gal like Terra that came for revenge for her father's sake. Because her father wanted someone elses wife to be his owned is so patheic and sinful. As Sam sat and stares at Terra's loud mouth he heard a train coming but didn't know which end it was coming from out of the west or the east. But it was coming quick and in a hurry. So Sam gather all his weapons to do battle if necessary. Suddenly the engine starts to slow down a bit but kept on going west with military equipement on flatbed cars. Sam had to go out on his back porch for a closer look at things so if Ed decides to run up on the property Sam can start shooting from a distant before getting to his back door or before reaching the barn and edge of the corn field. Now if Ed has Sheila with him Sam thought not to shoot at all. Sam doesn't want to make a fatal mistake in shoot his daughter. The shot must be on target to hit Ed.

Sam's thoughts hoping that his daughter is ok from her car accident and being out here with a lunatic like Ed. Now on thee other hand Ed is wandering where is his daughter he hasn't heard from her to see if she comply to his orders in killing both father and son. Now it's real late for Sam to be expecting someone to approach his door while sitting at the kitchen table ready to shoot anything that moves. As Terra started to knod in and out. Sam would be nice and lay her on his sofa but kept an eye on her. Afterward's laying Terra onto the sofa. Sam went back into the kitchen to fix a little bit of a breakfast for himself. With eggs sausage homefries and toast. As he sat and waited on his breakfast he received a weird phone call from another person that would just call and hang up. But no one will say anything on the other end.

Then Sam glances at his livingroom to see what Terra was doing. Then he would answer the phone. "Hello." Sam said.

Then he puts the phone back on the reciever. "Idiot!" said Sam. But Terra was still sleep or pretending to be sleep.So Sam sat where he could keep his eyes on her constantly.

Because to Sam Terra is a b-t-h to him. Once a b-t-h always a b-t-h. Sam is not taking any chances with her around him. If keeping one eye on his food and one eye onTerra that's what he going to do. Sam knows now that his slip up has cause him a lot of grief and pain by letting a well attracted and deranged looking girl into his and his children lives.

Now as Sam getting ready to eat his breakfast he thought of checking on Terra before sitting down to eat. Sam had to get a little closer to recognize that something looks wet on his sofa. Yeap. Terra's butt had urinated on the sofa to get back at Sam for not letting her use his bathroom when told.

"Your a lousy muthf$%&@! You! Pissed on my nice sofa damn you!!" Sam said. "Well! you should've let me use your bathroom you old ass moron!" said Terra. "Well I was going to offer your deranged ass some breakfast now you starve whore!" said Sam. "Shuck's! I don't want a damn! thing from you!" But to kill you!"Terra said. "Your old ass need to listen next time!" said Terra. As the formal couple has lost their patients with each other by calling names and trying to hurt each other in the process. Maybe there is still a connection with the two. But the mystery behind the phone calls has Sam a little worried. For someone to keep on calling then not to say a word would drive anyone crazy.

But it's very perculiar up until now. Ed has Sam's number forever the thing is that Ed maybe trying to see at what angle to come from. Which is very smart. See if Ed was a hired hand to kill someone he would be good at it.

Because you can find that angle to come from to get the job done. no matter what. But also Ed is very sloppy at what he does. He is also showing Sam a hateful surprise with his daughter being involved. And with Sam the feelings are mutual. There isn't no love lost for bring one anothers daughter into this modern day hate for each other.

All over a woman Ed thinks.June should've been absolutely his but kills her to get at her husband. Sam's ways of doing absolutly wrong towards Ed when they were young boy's that didn't understand between right and wrong.So Ed needs to pay retribution to Sam for doing what he knows best.

Sam use to having his way at anything and everything on the playground and the arcade. So Ed was always last and second fiddle to Sam and others. But rubing Ed in a sensitive way that Ed had bottle his hate for others and especiallyfor Sam. But boy's being boy's could make up at anytime. But now one means good and the other means evil. With as old as Sam knowing that he probably have forgotten about most of what happen when they were young. But all they can do is put it aside and move on. Ed of all people does not forget or show forgiveness. Like evil do is what evil does. More less a snake's nature is that to bite to defend itself for whatsoever or whosoever invades it's space. But peace stands alone with envying and strife opposing all that it can. As time places a part in both families lives it wanders if both girls will live or both fathers may end each others live. Something must take place to smooth things out among both fathers. Without the law getting involved. See Sam doesn't really know if Ed killed June. All Sam knows that Ed has his daughter. And Ed is thinking the same way about Sam having his daughter for a hostage. Because Ed haven't heard anymore from her. After he had gave her orders to go and kill the son first then his father. In all Terra was too clever for to be so young. Well look who she has gotten it from of course. But Sam has speculate that Ed is the reason why Jay is gone and June's disappearance and now he has Sheila for a hostage for what? Sam absolutely doesn't know. But mean time Sam is so ready to put all this behind him and move on.

With pouring salt on each others wounds Ed hasn't had enough and Sam is trying to move on passed everything. But this railway of deceitfulness has pulled him back in. With the gravitational pull of evil and hatred had lured Sam and his family into everything. But Sam knows self temperance meekness and humility for to overcome the war of hell and Ed. Now Ed still has Sheila with him on his locomotive in the rail yard twelve miles from his home going west in the opposite direction. But Sam has Terra at his place trying to keep from hurting her or trying hard enough not to put a bullet into her. So it has come cross Sam's mind to go to the nearest rail yard to look for trouble with Ed. Eventually Sam may find it there without any doubt in mind that his daughther Sheila may be there. But one problem is that Terra is with him so putting her butt in the back seat of the truck and drive to the nearest rail yard to find his daugther there to get her back. Sam's thoughts is that Jon be release from the hospital's as soon as possible. So Jon and him could go to together to find Ed and whipp the taste out of his mouth. For what he and his daugther had put the family through. But Sam still having tendencies to shoot the young girl he met at a clinic and fell in love with. And not knowningly she is Ed's daughther from a past relationship.

But whatsoever Sam is thinking of he is going to move as quickly and with no mercy. Because time isn't waiting for no man. And this creature is about to strike again to wipe the family out once and for all. But alignment with a father and son is about to once more put everything in perspected.

Now with Ed trying to align his day with ending Sam's life isn't going as pleasant as it should. As Sam get prepared to leave the house. What a surprise to see his son be dropped off by a cab. While Jon is trying to get out of the cab with his left arm in cask bandage up. But was glad to be back home. As Sam walks up to Jon and tell him that he love's him and Sheila so much. "Dad I never stop loving you matter what." Jon said. As they take a moment in embrace each other. Then Sam realize that he left Terra on the floor between the coffee table and sofa. Terra urinated on herself on Sam's sofa So Sam removed her off the sofa on to the floor. As walking in the front door Jon smile like it was his last. Because Terra was in between a soft place and a hard spot That made Jon's day to see her in restraints.

Laying there helpless crying and using profanity like a sailor. "All Bitch!

Shut the hell up!!" Jon said. "You tried to kill me and now look at your no good ass on the floor that's where you belong!!!" Bitch!!" said Jon. "Cmon Jonny Let's go and find your sister." Sam said. "I have a better idea let's put her sorry ass in the bed of the truck and take her with us."said Sam. "That way we can keep an eye on her and her father as well." Sam said. "What! Did you say!?" ask Jon. As Sam cut his eyes at his son to reveal the truth to his son for a net of safety. "Yes! She's Ed's daughter!" said Sam. "What! the hell!?" ask Jon. "I know I let this young girl into our lives but believe me I was wrong son to do that I hope you and your sister would forgive me." said Sam. "And one more thing Jon she's wasn't neither pregnant at all." said Sam. "She told me that her father sent her to kill me. But she had to eliminate you and sheila from thee equation to get to me." said Sam.

"That! No good heifer was lying to me the whole time!?" ask Jon. "But one thing is her dad and this creature are working together?" ask Sam. Now as both Sam and Jon think back in the previous months when this creature had exposed himself when he came for a fight with both men in the front yard of Sam's house. But both men was ever so clueless about fighting with a strange creature that no one else was supposed to know about. As the evening was about to end the men didn't have a clue on where to start looking for Sheila's whereabouts. So Sam thought maybe getting something out of Terra for a start and because two of them alone trying to comb a rural area would be impossible. So they thought on going back to Ed's home and wait for his arrival again. "That bastard! Has to come home sooner or later!" said Sam. "Wait a minute dad I got an idea." said Jon. As both men not realizing that Ed mght not show up as Ed "Dad! Let's take this heifer to her darn dad's house and wait until he gets there." said Jon. "You know I couldn't see this bulls#*t coming at all." Sam said. "And I couldn't imagine this kinda stuff happening also." said Sam. "But went we do see his freakin ass he's dog meat." said Jon. "Well Jonny i'm just glad to see you because if I had to stay another day with this tramp I would've shot her in the face then go to jail." said Sam.

"But dad if you would've shot her then Ed would have retaliated by shooting Sheila So don't do that." said Jon. "Well son your are right." Sam said. As both Sam and Jon getting ready to carried out their plans on handling Ed and getting Sheila back in one peace But a terrified turned is about to bring on much pain. Now as Jon was getting weapon's and ammo out of his closet he notice a lingering stinch outside of his bedroom window in which would make a man wanted to puke that's how strong it was. So Jon thought that he should go out to check around the house to see what could it be smelling so awful? Jon thought. As going out to check Jon grab his 9mm glock and his hunting knife that he can kill an elephant with. As he walks next to the house as slow to approached his enemy Jon was getting really nervous on seeing something he shouldn't be seeing. As he approach the backyard he could see two dead corpse one male and the other a female.

Jon yelled for his father. "Dad!!!" said Jon. As he stood there with one bad arm and a good arm on his pistle. He yelled again for Sam to come to the backyard. Well Sam was already in the kitchen coming to the back door to see why Jon is yelling at the top of his lungs. When Sam open the back door what a very very hateful surprise he got to see with a awful smell coming at him.

It was two dead and decaying corpse laying up near the house like someone or something just dumped them there. And it looks like that creature got a hold of them both. But the way it looks the corpse also being 4th degree burns all over their bodies are not reconizeable. But to Sam and Jon who could've did such a thing?

The creature or maybe Ed. "This is very sickening to look at." Sam said. "Dad! Look!" said Jon. "Those shoes looks a lot like your mom shoes." Sam said. As he starts to tear up. And Jon was getting a bit nervous cause the female could be June's body. As Jon rolled the female over on her back to get a good look at her face and it was her as Jon failed backward to the ground while both men cried. Sam failed to his knees next to June's corspe talking in a soft voice to let her know that he misses her and he still love her. As Jon sat there rocking back& forth looking on.

But both men have one thing in mind that is revenge revenge and revenge. For a mother's and wife's sake. Jon wants the creature and Sam wants Ed so bad he could taste it. Now both men pulled themselves together to see who was the other corpse. It's had a similar look also as Jon ask Sam "Who is this?" ask Jon. Sam helps Jon rolled the other corpse on it's back to get a look at and it's Jay Sam's son in law which was slice in so many laceration's it seems like he was tormented for being the in law to the Bentford's. "Man! This is insane! to see sh-like this in our backyard!" said Jon. "I can't wait anymore to get my hands on that damn creature!" said Jon."Well son we don't know specifically who did this far as i'm concerned Ed could've done this." said Sam. "So dad what our we going to do?" ask

Jon. "Since we can't get the authoritie involved." said Jon. "Jon maybe it's a good idea to get the sheriff here to look at this." Sam said. "Besides we aren't touching a thing." said Sam. "I hear you dad." Jon said. But not far off the creature was up in a tree over looking at the Bentford's place watching both Sam and Jon from a distance while they both wandering about the corpse it put there. This is how close death can linger from a dire distances. Before it move in for the kill. It's funny how life can show you many ways it can take you when not knowing it right there at your door.

As Sam and Jon walks to the back porch to go in make a call to the sheriff office to report the missing corpse on the property. But it gave both men something to think about Sheila's well being this long away from home. "Dad let me go and check up on this ruthless heifer." Jon said. While Jon making sure that Terra is still breathing with restraints on her legs and wrist to keep her from getting away or keep her from doing any damage whatsoever. And Sam walks over to the phone to call the sheriff to explaine that his late wife and son in law are in his backyard and they both needs to be bury soon. Because with them laying in the back of the house is reeking havac throughout the community. As Sam neighbor's start to look his way and wandering what in the heck is that awful stinch. But Sam pays them no mind. Even though Sam's neighbor's are a mile and a half up the road and down the road. But while Sam was on the phone talking with Sheriff Protzman he heard a train coming but didn't know which direction it's coming from. As Jon also heard it while in the front yard. Jon takes off into the house to see what will occur with this train.

As both men knew their routine for a stop train behind the house. That means expect a fight coming or it's passing through. Well this paticular train was very heavy. With 8 locomotives pulling a load of military equipement coke

(coal) automobile's chemical tankers and with a little bit of freight also. But no creature no Ed. By calling the Sheriff to let him know about the corpses that was in the backyard needs to be buried soon.

As the creature was about to make his move again here comes the authorities showing up at the house with the CSI group the media and Lajunta Investigation bureau. Now Sam's house is live and well over the corpses that's in his backyard. As deputies yellow tape the area off to keep the investigation from being tainted. While deputies and detectvies were questioning both Sam and Jon on why are these corpses in this yard? But no one seems to know anything.

But thee culprit is standing by to strike again waiting for everything to clear. Because if it would strike now with law enforcement there with a lot of firearms at hand it would lose. That would be to many guys to fight off. And everyone has a weapon to kill. But the creature only wants the family that all and that's it. With the day being awfully hot some of the detectives complainted about the grossness of the smell that had some gaging for air and one deputy regurgitate in the corner of the yard. As Sheriff Protzman aproaches Sam ask if he could talk to him alone. "Sam I know that is June lying there isn't it?" asking Sheriff Protzman.

As Sam started to tear up again with revenge in his eyes to get the ignorance of envy malice lasciviousness hated emulations and there isn't any love for the equation. But in a soft tone Sam's acknowledgement for the question that the sheriff ask him. "Yes it's her." said Sam. "Oh dear God have mercy." Sheriff said. "Well I might as well assume that my daughther will show up this way." said Sam. "Sam don't say that please!" said Sheriff. "And by the way who is that in the back of your truck?" ask Sheriff Protzman.

"Jonny's ex's girlfriend." said Sam. "Jon's ex! Tied up like that!?" ask Sheriff Protzman. "ok! Sam what aren't you not telling me?" asking the Sheriff. "Look Sheriff there's my boy over there so why don't you go and ask him." Sam said.

"You don't mind I will." said Sheriff. "Jon Bentford! why is there a female in restraint's in the back of your truck?" ask the Sheriff. "Well Sheriff to keep her from misbehaven all day." said Jon. "I'm getting ready to take her into the house and make love to her."said Jon. "Ok you do just that and take those retraint's off please!" said the Sheriff. While the law enforcement are hanging around. Sam and Jon both was very close in getting caught with having Terra in the back of the truck and having the corpses in the backyard.

Therefore none of this wasn't call for. And Sam wasn't to call the authority to get them involve. That's not Sam's intentions to dragged the Sheriff in it. This is a fight to the finish. Jon wants the creature for his mother brother in law sake. As Sam needs a piece of Ed and the creature for revenge for his wife sake. Both men are about to get what they both being craving for. Is a fight to kill. This really doesn't have to be this way. But Ed made this like it is. As Jon tried to bring Terra into the house She starts to yelled for help. "Hey! Please someone help me they are trying to kill me!!!" said Terra. As Jon gags her mouth. But none of the lawmen pay any attention to her. Sheriff Protzman just left to go to another accident near the expressway. Which both Sam and Jon was glad to see him go. Because Sam thinks Sheriff Protzman isn't serious enough about his job.

But he would take the salary if a baby would offer it to him.

The Soft Reckeoning

Chpt XVI

As the day comes to an end while all the authority figures are still on the site. Here comes a train out of the west.Coming on strong with loads of automobile's aluminum and sheet metal. With 6 Locomotive's pulling and non stop. Sam and Jon stood in the middle of the yard to see what's about to occur. While detective's and deputies are out in thee opening. "Jonny Let's see if this sucker would try some trick or other with all these guy's are still here." Sam said. "If so it's ready to die then" Jon said. But the train kept on going for it's destination until it was completely out of sight. "I wished it would come here while these guy's are here" said Jon. "Naw it's smarter then that with all these guy's still walking around here."Sam said. "It's wants a fight with as little than a crowed." Jon said. That creature seems very intelligence to knowningly right from wrong. And knows when to come around when theres no one else is around.

Now Sheila is still missing with Ed. And Sam with Jon are waiting on this creature to show up in a moment for a fight.

Therefore go and chase down Ed and put a bullett in his head for all this mess he had cause. As Jon had thought.

Because of law enforcement is about to leave and the C.S.I and Corner offices has the two corpses and leaving also. Now that the crowd has disburse all at once it's back to Sam and Jon by themselves now for the creature to move for the kill. As everything and everyone is gone. Theres a train that is moving a little slower on the far set of rails to get a look at Sam's backyard to come in the back door. Now the locomotive is half way down the track. Look who it is it's the creature in it's form with a nasty stare at the Bentford's house ready to go in and do some damage more like killing. As it makes it way to the house to see if both men are inside to go in and fight with who ever willing to die first. As it stood at the back porch grawling in a ferocious way to come out and fight with it. Surprisely Sam and Jon had left with Terra in the bed of the truck. Going and trying to find Sheila. Before it get any later.

The Creature tearing the back door down to get in as it starts to walks throughout the house. Looking for Sam or Jon or both it wants to destroy as bad as it smells. So what does it do instead? It takes it's anger out on the house and everything that's in it's way. The Creature throwed furniture rip the sink off of kitchen wall it put large holes in the walls. It throwed small objects through the windows. This Creature is so violent and so out of control with one mis sion to do was come and destroy and leave casualities behind. It's just tee off cause Sam isn't where he needed to be so it can finished Sam off and Jon too.

The house is in a total wreck and salivate everywhere the house stank real bad with this creature in it.

Therefore if Jon and Sam would returned quickly they can catch it Before it decides to leave. But one last thing it did do was ripped the family portrait off of the wall. As it goes out the way it came leaving the Bentford's home in a wreck it walks back to it's locomotive and backs up going the way it came. Leaving a serious messenge that it was there. It's wants a war to the finished. It's like David and Goliath all over again but there are a lot of differences here. As weapons and the creature has special abilities to make itself invisible move objects with a glance. It's eyes can see like a hawk and talons like a eagle height 7'6. The best way is to blow it's knee caps out to get it to a level for to be beatin stabbed and then shot.

Meanwhile Sam and Jon rode to the next county over for to getting information on Ed's home. But the place closes at 6:30pm. It's 8:00pm. "Well we will tried it tomorrow son." Sam said. "Let's go by his house to see if he's home."

Jon said. "Well it want hurt to check to see if this prick is around or at home." Sam said. As driving to Ed's residences Sam notice that theres a locomotive sitting on the far rails near and between Booker road and Newport lane. But one thing is missing the writing on the locomotive that tells you to take a ride to hell. But Sam still check it out anyway to see if Ed was on board. As Sam drove alone this dirt path near the track bed he saw two older gentleman's having a smoke while talking with one another. But Sam had thought's to just keep on driving. But he still stop to ask a couple of questions. "Excuse me gentlmen do you guys knows a Edward Dart?" ask Sam. One of the men just looked at Sam liked he said something wrong and the men did ask "who is that?" Then and there Sam knew that Ed isn't seems to be who he really is. As Sam getting back into the truck to take off here comes the Sheriff with more qu estions about the corpses on how long were they there? But Sam couldn't tell them anything So they came at Jon.

Because Jon is the one that had found his mother and Brother in law lying in the backyard still considerabley decomposing with the time he discovered them. All Jon say he said was he had smell this bad odor near his bedroom window. As Jon telling and explaining how he had discovered his mom and brother in law's corpses being in the backyard.

But Jon as well as Sam couldn't tell the authorities much more then what had happened but the question is how they got there and who put them there? And both Sam and Jon knows who did what. But not telling who did what. Jon's mind said that the creature and Sam's thought's are that Ed had a play in this situation. So therefore both father and the son are on the same page. Of course both men are right but one thing is one can't function without thee other in this matter. Because the two are one and Sam and Jon doesn't quite knows that for sure. Ed had almost exposed himself to the family once in previous months by coming to the house with a wounded leg. From Sam's gun when he shot the creature in the leg the night it fought with the family in the front yard. So Ed wanted to kill the Bentford's for that mishave. If Ed exposed himself to Sheila then Sheila is so dead. Because Ed doesn't want the people to know what his evil side looks like. Because the creature kills at will once discovered. A evil individual doing dirty in a Satanic works. See people would say often be careful at what you would ask for. Because they would believed that they can received it and not knowningly it's could be very harmful to their health. Therefore Ed did ask for this and wasn't thinking that this situation could've killed him instead.

Like people companies and organizations they all have to function with one thing in mind money! Like everyone has that one thing in common that is a big amount on life itself. Big house nice set of wheels big bank account and all of this is in vain or vanity. With all of this Ed's doing is in vain. Ed wanted the biggest killing machine there was a train locomotive that could damaged hurt and also kill if anything is in it's way. Now Ed needed a well developed creature also that could do his evil works for him. That has abililies to disappeared see far jump and kill without anyone knowning it's him that is behind this creature.

Now with the weather is changing drastically to cold over night. Ed had turned to his normal self. Taking Sheila to a nearby hideout to keep her from freezing. Ed can't transformed in front of Sheila Ed has to get out of sight before he could turned from man to beast. Again if he is seen changing from beast to man he must kill them instant. So they only see him in one form beast or man. "Man! You stinks!"

Sheila said. "Silence! Before I throw you in that hole over there." Ed said. There was a large hole to where he puts his other unknowns he had killed with the locomotive by taking their remaine's and burned them into ashes. But Sheila thought of trying to get a loose to see her whereabouts so she can high tail it from this derange lunatic of a man. To Sheila Ed is gets creepy by the seconds. Sooner of later Ed would need to eat to keep his enter utmost calm. His eyes would turned a slight color then normal sort of like a diabetic when it's sugar is low or high that Ed's way that he needs to eat.

Ed also has a weakness it is that he can't be around water to long. Water makes his pors to open and this makes him very vulnerable to the air and water. See the creature knows when it sees water it tenitive to run into the opposite direction to keep from getting harm. While Ed is trying his best to get close to Sheila because she reminds him of June so much when he looks at her. "Hey have anyone ever told you that you look like your mom?" huh? ask Ed. Sheila just ignored him. With a pissed off look. Then Ed started touching Sheila's cold feet and legs as she trying to come undone with her hands tied behind her. But in Ed's head he wants to seduce Sheila so bad that his lust is coming undone with a weird smirk on his face as he also drool at the mouth.

For to make a move on this young lady. "Not on your best day you will never tasted this!" Sheila said. "My father and brother is going to kill your weird ass for sure messing with me!" Sheila said. "Far and utmost your family is already dead for as i'm concerned." Ed said. "Mr. Dart why are you doing this to us?" Sheila asking. "Like I said before your father has being a thorn in my side for decades with misery!" Ed said. "Does it occur to you that dad might have forgotten all about what had happen between you and him?" Sheila asking. "Look here sweetheart I have a memory like a elephant so I don't forget." Ed said. "So what should I do? Just lay down and act like nothing happen?"

Ed asking. "Shut up! Before I kill you here and now." said Ed. "So you going to kill me? And what does that prove?"

Sheila asking. "It proves you are dead! Decease! No more! That's what that means!" said Ed.

As Ed gets upset with Sheila for trying to talk some sense into him to where he doesn't want to hear anything positive coming from a younger woman that he is trying his best to seduce her while he has her in his hands. Ed is thinking when Sheila goes to sleep that's his cue to get next to her.

But time is against Sam and Jon trying to find Sheila quick and in a hurry. Before Ed could make Sheila a mom and Sam a grandfather. Sheila hasn't seen Ed as a creature. So Ed could kill Sheila if he have any type of sexual intercourse because of his DNA can't mixed with hers. Knowing Ed he doesn't care as long as he can stick to her for pleasure.

Therefore Sheila was very beautiful and well groom by her mother on how to be a lady. With long brown hair her eyes are hazel green her stature is 5'3 and 117lbs with a gorgous figure. So that's why Ed would like to lay with her. Two people comes to mind with Ed is Terra's mom Terri and June when looking at Sheila. As Sheila lay's helpless on a dirty floor determine to work herself loose in which is hard to do with her hands tied behind her and her legs are restrainted as well. "Hey are you hungry!?" asking Ed. As Sheila ignored him. Now Ed goes and starts touching Sheila on her leg and then her foot. "Damn it! Man! I already told you do not touch me!!"said Sheila. With a mean look in her eyes.

"You are nothing but a horny old bastard!!" Sheila said. As Ed tried to stick himself to Sheila's behind when he lifted her off of the floor on to the chair." I was just trying to help you up you bitter bit--!" Ed said. "i don't need you helping me up Because all you want is a taste some kind of way!" Sheila said. Now that Sheila had told Ed about himself he knows that this young girl is onto his actions as a dirty old man that wants to mess around with young girls. But Ed had thoughts differently of killing Sheila and dumping her body in the backyard as well. But Ed thinks it's not to late to considerabley go as planned. By turning to his dark erside and then kill Sheila that way. And put her body on the locomotive and dragged her through the corn field onto the back yard. But before anything to take place Ed is still wants to mess with her while she's his prisoner.

But meantime Jon and Sam was headed back to the house when they passes Ed's place but still no sign of Ed neither Sheila. So they kept going. But they have notices that theres a locomotive sitting further down the tracks near a signal like it's waiting on something. As both men decides to check it out driving passed the house looks a little unusaul with broken glass all over the porch and items on the ground. So both men pulling up in the driveway of the house to see what had happen. As leaving Terra in the bed of the truck. First thing is first. Both men had grab their weapons from the back seat of the truck. Because the windows has being shattered the back door is off of it's hinges holes in the walls and the furniture is destroyed the kitchen sink is off the wall the place has being ram sack. "Wow! Who in the f—k could do this!?" asking Jon. While Sam had a miserable look and a hurt feelings about the house him and June had built is wrecked in pieces.

But Sam and Jon notices a scent with salivate everywhere the creature had paid a visit but no one was at home. "That muth@#*&^! I can't wait no longer that's it!!" Jon said.

"Jon! wait a second you can't fight this creature with one arm boy you need to think first." Sam said. "Now it's going to take the two of us to get the job done."Sam said. "Again, I don't want to loose you again Jon." Sam said. "Dad! I'm just so tired of this sh--! i'm ready for a damn war!" said Jon. "Son! really! that thing is trying to lure us in as much as possible." Sam said. Now Sam knows 100% in the back of his mind that this creature is working with Ed. And Sam know he's not in the best of shape to fight with anything.

But Jon must prove himself as a man of valor for the family sake. But Jon is biting off more then he can chew going after both Ed and the creature. All by himself can be a little extreme to fight with a creature with powers of destruction with one good arm at that Jon will die.

"Ok! Dad what about that locomotive up the tracks just sitting there?" Jon ask. As both men taking a closer look at a locomotive sitting far off from the house. While having a conversation as both men strolled through the corn field to get to the tracks. But by the time they got there the locmotive had moved on. "Damn it!! it's gone!" Jon said. Back through the corn field they goes. But before they can reach the back porch of the house. Both men looked at each other they both heard the same sound of a engine coming their way as both men were waiting near the porch with weapons in hand. To see what may transpired. "Dad are you going to be ok?" ask Jon. Sam didn't response right away while checking his weapon to see if it was loaded. "Yes son I be ok." Sam said. As the locomotive was slowing down a bite both men aims at the locomotive just in case the creature or Ed might try some sort of trickery. But as Jon thought it wasn't even close it was a passenger train coming through non stop. Sam and Jon looked at one another and smile Because it could've being worse for both sides right there and right now. It's wasn't meant to be with Sam's heart beating in his chest like he just got off of a treadmill from doing a couple of miles. And Jon also wasn't ready to confront the creature with one bad arm. If Jon misses his target that could be his life if the creature lay his claws on Jon. Mean while Ed is still thinking on killing Sheila and put her corpse on the property just as he did Mrs. Bentford and Sheila's husband Jay. And Ed had thoughts again of killing her in the presence of transforming from man to beast. Another way that Ed had thought to kill Sheila was to throw her in front of the locomotive and run her over behind her house.

Therefore Ed's sickness with his evil entity really has a hold on his life for all of those innocent individual's from the past up until now those souls will haunt Ed dead or alive. While sitting in front of Sheila revealing all that he could say to her on how he's so obsessed with evil towards other people including her parent's. That evil spirit came upon him in a unusal way. "Your mother was my girlfriend before your ugly a-daddy came into the picture!" said Ed. "Look who's talking you got some nerves calling my father ugly because i'm staring ugly and miserable in the damn face!" said Sheila. "Silence!! I don't want to hear another word out of you!! is that understood!?" ask Ed. "You just don't know how much I would love to kill you right here right now!" said Ed. "I didn't mean to kill your mother I needed to get your mother away from him so we could be together!" said Ed. "Up until this day I still love your mother." said Ed. "So why did you killed her then!?" ask Sheila. Ed just went silence. While Sheila couldn't hold back her tears over how her mother death wasn't necessary. By listening to a luntic of a man that needs help desperately bad. "I'm sorry that your mother were in the wrong place at the wrong time." said Ed.

As Sheila wept bitterly and couldn't forgive Ed if she wanted too. Therefore Ed has taken her mother's life over a bitter rivalry that happen many years ago between her father and Ed as kid's. "Ed! You will have karma on the porch at the door staring you in the face." said Sheila. "O yeah! like I care if karma showed up on my door step! Who f—king care! You care!? I don't care! Because babygirl it happened oh well! it is what it is!" said Ed. And again i'm sorry! For killing your mom and husband!" Ed said.

Now therefore Sheila really wept over the two people that she really misses much is her husband Jay and her mother, June. Which they shouldn't died. But Ed is going to received what he shall deserve. As Sheila thought. As Ed pace back and forth to think on his next plans to go and confront Sam and Jon for a show down as himself or with his arsenal the creature. As he started to think out loud for Sheila to hear what is about to happen is this. "Damn it! I know what I'm about to do! How about this a even trade for you and get your father." said Ed. "Let you go for your daddy." So how about those apples!?" ask Ed. Sheila just gaze at stupidity like a worthless idiot trying to walk without legs.

But back at Sam's place they are still trying to clean up the place from the creature's havac. So Jon when outside to pulled Terra from the bed of the truck as she lay helpless in the cold wind shaking like a leaf on a tree. Jon yell's for his dad to give him a hand to dragged this big mouth woman in to the house. "Dad!! I need a hand!" said Jon. "How much I would love to leave her retarded a-out here in this cold weather I really do!" said Jon. "Son no! We aren't doing that." Sam said. "Let's take her in and laid her next to the fireplace. Sam said. As Terra started to get real lippy with both men she held her tongue. Because she was to cold to speak back anything negative.

When both men had gotten Terra inside and laid her next to the fireplace so she can stay warm. Both men look each other in thee eyes cause a sound of a train was coming. So they lay Terra on the floor then grab their weapons and headed back to the back yard just in case something didn't look right from a distance. They didn't know what to expect a man or creature or maybe both. Both Jon and Sam knows to be prepared to handle business to protected what's matters most that is family. Surprise it was a single locomotive going down the tracks slowly at one point it looks like it wants to stop directly behind the house. As Jon thought of taking a closer look to see who's on board but it's very risky to get to close to the tracks. Therefore both men are looking for one or thee other to come shooting or swinging like an out of control lunatic. "Hey Dad! That looks like Ed there!" said Jon. As both men started walking as fast as they could towards the tracks to get him off of the locomotive to give his a-a beating for all of the problems he has cause for this family. Ed needs to feel the repercussions of a bullitt in the temple. As Jon thought standing there near the tracks. While Sam looking for a complete stop down the tracks. And Sam had thought right for the locomotive did stop down the tracks. "Jon! Cmon son!" said Sam. The locomotive did stop as it gotten further down the tracks. So Sam and Jon both are going to see for themselves what's up with this locomotive without any cargo or freight. So they wants Sheila back that's all. While Ed just seeking revenge for years of envy and jealousy. As Sam tells Jon to take one side of the locomotive Sam takes on thee other side. "If it's the creature you start blasting!" Sam said. "Ok dad!" said Jon.

By the time the men has gotten to the locomotive they were out of breath but that didn't stop them from coming to do what needed to be done. As surrounding the locomotive Jon saw a older gentleman standing to the side of the tracks smoking a cigar minding his own business until he saw a couple of men with gun's. As the older gentleman put his hands up with a frighting look thinking he was being rob for his wallet or the locomotive not knowing anything about the area. Until Sam started talking and apologized for drawned weapons on him. "Mister my son and I are very sorry for scaring you like this. We just trying to find my daughter and this looks like the locomotive that sats down at thee other end of the tracks." Sam said. "Well guys i'am new to this area so I couldn't tell you anything if it would save my life.

So i'm sorry as well for not being much help." Gentleman said. "You guys have a good day." said the gentleman. "Sir you do as well." Sam said.

Then the gentleman took off slowly down the tracks which a train was coming going in the opposite direction pulling freight behind it. As both Sam and Jon stood far off observing the passing locomotive to see if Ed is on it. By evening it started to get real cold as fall came quick. As both men just stood there looking up and down the tracks just hoping that Ed would show up or the creature in case. For a real good fight. This will be a fight to the finished. A friend versus friend and no loss to Ed but Sam has something to loses and that is a miss guilded and wicked friendship that was and now it wasn't a friendship after all. As both Sam and Jon headed back to the house they both noticed that the barn door was hanging again So Sam when into the house to get his hammer and screwdriver to put the door back up. While Jon goes and start removing old screws and nails. Jon looks inside of the barn there was a scent that could make a dead man stand and walk.

But Jon wasn't going in alone he waited for his father to returned before he would go any further. Sam returned looking at Jon's face expression. "What now Son?" ask Sam. "Oh you doesn't smell that dad?" ask Jon. "Well the barn has being shut for awhile." said Sam.

Meanwhile Ed still has his mind full of the lust on getting next to Sheila. So finally Sheila had a great thought on how to used her body to get her out of the situation. Sheila did the unthinkable. Sheila knows as a woman on how to get into a guy's brain. By using body language and draw the guy to you. "Hey Eddie can I have somethin to drink?"ask Sheila. "Whoa! What did you call me!?"ask Ed. "Eddie." said Sheila. "No one has called me that in years!" said Ed. "I like it it's sexy and it holds a lot of meaning." said Sheila.

"Well Eddie! do you like cake or something sweet!?" ask Sheila. As Ed standing there looking so goofy and speakless with a slight wood in the pants. "Eddie come here and taste a little of me for this is what you wanted all alone. Right!?" ask Sheila. Ed had a grin from ear to ear waiting for the moment to feel good once again as a kid wanting cake and milk before dinner. But Ed watch Sheila as she sat in the chair with only a hospital's gown on. With her legs slightly opened for Ed to get his eyes quite full for everything to work with momentum. As Sheila starts her horny side to get Ed's brains to where he would make a fatal mistake for not thinking with his brain instead the one between his legs is thinking in high gear. As Sheila thought if she could slightly seduce Ed she could make her move. But she must tired him out to make him to where she could grab his clothes and split. Sheila knows it's cold but she has to make a sacrifice and endurance the cold weather with just a hospital's gown. Now she's feeling quite strong to get Ed to do what she needs for him to do. As Ed down on his knees to undo the restraints that is holding Sheila's leg's together.to loosen for pleasure as Ed breathe with excitement like a child on christmas day trying to opened his presents in a hurry." Wow girl this is all I being thinking about you! Sh--!" said Ed.

But one thing Ed hasn't realized that Sheila's restraint's for her hands are loosen as well. But he pulled Sheila's body to the edge of her seat to get next to her. As Sheila eyes behold Ed's eyes for her to grab the metal bar that's next to the chair to hit him as hard as she can so she can get out of there.

And run for help. "Eddie! You like that baby it feels so good you go boy!" said Sheila. While Ed was between Sheila's legs she notices the smell he had on him and the large hole in his leg that all of this is coming to her remembrance the night that her brother and father had a fight with the creature in the front yard. Ed smells just like the creature as Sheila thought.

Now that Ed is having so much fun with a gorgous girl like Sheila and not knowing she is playing the role to bash Ed's skull in. But also Sheila is playing on dangerous grounds with Ed's evil intelligence. As Ed humps on this young beautiful girl like crazy while she lays there for a moment for Ed to feel good about being a horny no good stinken ass bastard. As Sheila thought. (Thump!) As Sheila hits Ed in the head. She stood there for a second thinking what to do next as she runs to the door but it has a lock on it Now Ed is knockout cold while Sheila is struggling to get out.

There is a window that is boarded up. This little shack isn't big at all. With one door and a window there is another room with a window. As Sheila takes the metal bar she hit Ed with to get out by beating the glass out of the window. She may cut herself but she is getting out of there. Before Ed can come to his senses Sheila is making it out the window.

Just as Sheila's heel of her foot reaches the window seal. Ed grabs it trying to pull her back in. But Sheila started kicking like crazy. But she hit the cold cement hard. But Ed. runs quickly the door to goes out to get his prey. By the time that Ed got outside Sheila hid in the bushes as she tremble in the cold. "Sheila! Cmon babe! and let's finished what you and I had started!" Ed said. As Sheila remained silent for how long with it being so cold out. As it gotten dark and cold Sheila can died from the cold weather. "Sheila!! it's cold out here so cmon back and I let you live!" said Ed. Now Sheila had made it to the road for help.

The thing is to get someone to stop for help. But for Sheila no problem for a beautiful girl only have on a hospital's gown and barefoot. Reaching out for help as quickly as possible. As Ed decided to walk towards the road to see if he could see Sheila insight. "There's that bitch." said Ed. As Sheila kept on walking until someone passes by and not look to see who's is behind her but she heard foot steps and Sheila took off running to the next house she came up on screaming as loud as she could for help. Ed stop chasing her and head back to that shack of his to get his evil side to go and to do damage. As a elderly lady was passing Sheila she stop to see if she could be any help to her. And Sheila ran to her the elderly lady help Sheila into the car to get her to a hospital but Sheila told her no hospital. "Please! Take me home! please ma'am take me home." said Sheila. "Who was that man chasing you?" asking the elderly lady. As the elderly lady help Sheila on into her car. Before the elderly could reach her drivers side door Ed had gotten to her By spliting her skull completely opened. Sheila Screaming at the top of her voice while locking the doors to keeping Ed from getting to her. As watching Ed from a distance Sheila can see that transfiguration in Ed. As Ed turning from man to a dog face like creature then he would make himself invisible. Which made Sheila keep on screaming like crazy.

Because as he walks he suddenly disappeared right into thin air. But you can hear him nearby and also smell his awfulness in which could make a skunk puke. Now Sheila is in the car but the keys are on the elderly lady's in the coat pocket on her dead body. When stopping for Sheila the lady tooking the keys with her for security reasons. So Sheila needs to move or freeze to death. But too scared and also shooken up at the dead lady lying next to the car or Ed's disappearing act. Either way Sheila has to get to Haskins road to where there's a lot of traffic and people all over the place that could help her in every way. It's getting colder by the seconds and Sheila will suffer from hypothermia if she waits any longer her heart will have troubles later on in life.

But as Sheila attempts to search the vehicle for keys so she doesn't need to go outside of the car for Ed to get her.

As she cried her tears started to freeze. It was impossible for her move like she wants too. But as it gotten down in the teens the windchill feels like zero weather. Without any type of clothing on Sheila came across a blanklet to cover herself. It's been awhile since she heard anything from Ed around the car. But when she had looked out to see the elderly lady her body was frozen solid. "If I could just get those keys off of her." Sheila thought. As Sheila attempts to get the keys from the dead elderly lady a bump from something up against the vehicle. So Sheila sat real still to see if it will do it again. The windows are frosted up so you can't see out.

But Sheila can hear foot steps around the vehicle. "Sheila! Sheila!! Sheila!! c'mon let's finished what we started and I let you go home after we are done!" Ed said. "Since I can't have your mother! I take you instead!" Ed said. "That pervert of a bit--." Sheila thought. As Ed being a horny man towards Sheila to get her back so he could finished having sex. But he doesn't want any sex. Ed is ready to kill Sheila and Sheila is a smart girl not to give in so quickly.

Now Sheila knows that she is about four miles out from the house. It's the cold that has her in one place like any other woman that don't like cold weather. But so happened that Sheila decides to lay still on the front seat. Until she put her hand under the seat and found a gun and key. The gun was loaded and the key fitted the ignition. Sheila still played it cool until she has enough energy to start the car.

"Sheila! please! Let me in babe! and if you don't let in I swear things is about to get even uglier!" said Ed. Sheila put the key in and try starting it. "Oh sh-- the battery." Sheila thought. Now the creature is on the scene

Ed has changed into the creature. The creature rams the car until it almost put it on it's top with Sheila inside crying to stay alive. But she must do something that she doesn't approve of that is to shoot anyone. But the creature must go. With only six shots, Sheila would have to utilized each bullitt to where it counts.

Sheila knows that if she misses that her life is over. (pow!! pow!!). Sheila lets off a couple of shots with one hit the creature's shoulder and the other grazed it's neck. Now with that Sheila made it also mad until it started ramming the car as hard as it can. Putting dents and knocking the glass out of the windows. To where it can reach in and grab Sheila out of the car.

The Creature is furious Because it is wounded again. Now it's intended to kill Sheila for shooting at it. Therefore walking around the vehicle multiple times grawling as loud as it can. But not far off is Jon taking the trash out putting it in the trash can next to the porch. Suddenly Jon heard that same grawling from far off just like over the way. As sticking his head in the back door to call his father. "Dad!Come here!"

Jon calls. Sam rushes to the back door to see what's up. "hey son what's a matter?" ask Sam. "listen." said Jon. "That's the same sound the night that we fought with the creature in the front yard." said Jon. Then Sheila let off another shot to wounded it some more the grawling got louder.

"Dad! What if that's Sheila?" ask Jon."Well sh--! lets check it out and make sure that we have plenty ammo." Sam said.

"That could be that funky a-creature." Jon said.Now Sheila is holding it off until her brother and father shows up. Now fire works are going to flied. As Sheila lets off another shot to tried getting the car started as well. Sheila only has two bullitts left. The creature has made it's way into the car to get Sheila out then she lets another shot and this one struck it's chest to weaken it a bit. Sheila is about out of breath fighting this creature off of her. It kept on coming matter what she did to it. Sheila has gotten colder and weaker from the creature over powering her to kill her.

Now that Jon and Sam are on their way to this scene for an encounter with this creature and Ed. They also needs some insurance as well with Terra's presence. As both men trying to pinpoint the shots and grawling noise they hurried out the door as soon as possible to catch it. So Jon help his father to get Terra into the cab of the truck. And Jon took off running in the direction of the shooting and grawling.

And Sam took off driving like a bat out of hell. All Sam can picture in his head that Sheila is fighting for her life and Jon wants the creature all to himself. (Pow!!) Sheila shot the final bullitt into the creature's chest and then it clawed her shoulder. Sheila started running around the car to stay away from it. Then it decide to go invisible on her to confused her and to catch her.

Sheila gets emotional because she sees her brother running to help her. As her shoulder bled like crazy. But she didn't care about her shoulder all that matter is seeing her brother in the distance aiming at the creature. Then Sheila ran to her father's truck as the creature ran behind her. Jon fires a shot and blew the right arm off (boom!!) (boom!!) another arm. The creature's grawling turns to squeeling as Jon gets close range for a head shot. "This is for all the problems you cause me and my family!" (boom!!). Jon blew half of the creature's brain onto the ground. But that didn't stop it from being aggressive still. Because it still moved around and half of it's body was invisible showing half man half beast. As the Bentford's stood and watches this creature goes from one to thee other was very sickening. Even Terra didn't know what to think seeing her father's evil side come to life.

In which he had a evil parasite growing decades inside of him. Until it took his evil and hatred and bottle the two into a deadly cocktail. This is what a small town had to go up against from losing innocent lives the pass years. No one couldn't figure out why so many good people were killed.

Ed had a lot of people fooled especially the Bentford's. It seems that the creature still have some life left in it. As it lying there with a hole in it's head with a slight grawl and orange like plasma running out of it. In Jon's mind was to finished it by putting another slug into it. But Terra spoke, "Please! He's no more harm!" said Terra. While she act in a emotional state. Sheila left her dad's arms to approach the young girl Terra to give her a hug. But Sheila did the unthinkable thing that was to punch Terra and draw kick her to the ground. "Bit--!!" said Sheila. Then Sheila gave her fatther a dirty look with a question. "Why in the hell! would you bring this whore! into our lives!?" huh!?"ask Sheila.

As Sam walks over to Sheila and apologized for the inconvenience it cause his kids. And putting them all in jeopardy.

"Hey honey i'm so sorry for what I have done but I hoping that you could find it in your heart to forgive me." said Sam. While everyone was talking and standing looking at the creature someone had called the authoritie Because of the shotgun blast.they heard. Suddenly the creature was turning back into Ed as it laid there without arms still squeeling to get up. Afterward's the spell wore off and Ed transformed back to himself with Sam a bitter look and goes over and starts kicking the man while he's down and dying. "Enough!! my father isn't anymore harm to you people so stop kicking him!!" said Terra. "Shut up Bit--!!" said Sheila. "Your damn daddy tried to kill me and then seduce me too!!" said Sheila. "Like father like daughter!" said Jon.

The county Sheriff department pinpoint where all the comotion was coming from Morgan Rd to where theres notthing but a rundown shack that belongs to the Taylor family in which they also died by the hand of Ed as well. Now that Sheriff Protzman is on the scene he is looking for answers on what had happened.

The Sheriff walks over to the Bentford's started with Jon.

But Jon didn't give him what he wanted to hear. "Sheriff! We just did your job for you." said Jon. "Yeah! Like hell! You just committed a crime son!" said Sheriff Protzman. "Hold it right there Sheriff! that man thats lying in front of you is the criminal he kidnapped my daughter and seduce her and his daughter trying to get me and as well as my son as well so who is the criminal now?" ask Sam. "Wait a minute! This is Ed Dart I thought you both were great friends?" ask the Sheriff. "That's what you get for thinking that." said Sam.

"Therefore where is the daughter?" ask the Sheriff. "There's that bit--! Over there!" said Sheila. "You better take her a way before I put her down with her daddy!" said Sheila.

"Sheila calm down sweetie." said Sam. "Dad! Don't tell me to calm down you know that I don't like her and then you going to let her take the place of my mother!!!" said Sheila.

Sheila left her father side to goes to her brother side as she tremble in the cold wind. "Ok! Who is that elderly lady lying there?" ask the Sheriff. "She came to rescue me and Ed killed her." said Sheila. "So! That's her car I take it?" ask the Sheriff. "yes!" said Sheila. "Ok. Listen I just ran a wrap sheet on Ed's daughter and she is wanted for the murders at Dr. Letchell office she killed the doctor and apparently the four nurses so she is a wanted individual." said the Sheriff. "Wow! That bit-- was busy!" said Jon. "She was trying to kill me too and then tried to entraped me as well!" said Jon.

"Hey Sam! Why don't you and your children's go home and get out of this cold weather and we take it from here." said the Sheriff. A Deputy went over to place Terra in custody for the crimes she had done and with her father gone she may change the game in her own vendetta with his gene's inside of her is a lot of evil growing to take over in latter years to come. Who knows that Terra could get off with a lighter sentences for her evil works she carried out for her father's sake. In the Book of Ecclesiastes shows that "Because sentence against an evil work is not executed speedily therefore the heart of sons of men is fully set in them to do evil.

In Ed's way he could get words out of you with his evil side. And Sam a kindful heart won his family back. But see Ed was watching and wanted thee weaker vessel of his plan without anyone knowning what he was up too. For years Ed couldn't keep his eyes off of June and neither young Sheila cause like mother so be the daughter as well. But going with June in his earlier years before Sam came alone and took June by surprise. That didn't sit well with Ed as June's boyfriend at the time. So Ed thought killing June would break Sam completely. And since he couldn't have her Sam couldn't have her neither. As people would often say keep your friends close but keep your enemies closer. So Ed did just that with Sam. The Bentford's are trying to adjust to each others pain's from the evil that came close to destroying a tight knitted family. And as humility help this family thru tragedy and triumph to stick together.to overcome the evil one's.

The Way it Wasn't

Chpt XVII

Now the house is needing a makeover by getting rid of some damages the creature had destroyed unless Sam wanted to have it restored. But for both Jon and Sheila thought other wise by getting new furniture and a kitchen makeover as well. But Sam wanted to take some of June's belonging and give away to someone who needs them. As winter weather is ushered in with a light snow fall and everyone's doing a little something to the house. Now Sheila is cleaning the livingroom and bathroom while both Sam and Jon working on the doors and windows with a lot of damaged to the kitchen. Sam realized that his insurance can take care at what he can't cover out of pocket. As continuing to get the house back in order there were dead spots at times when no one wouldn't speak for five to ten minutes to each other.

As reality has set in with each one in a different way (that this just happened) or (did that really just happened?) On the night that June's disappearance took place was a nasty taste in Sam's mouth. As Sam thinks of June's smiles and just being a impeccable wife to him and a execellent mother to his offsprings. Sam has a ruff time in accepting June's absence and a big void in his life. But it's hard to move ahead without the one you love. Jon knows on thee other hand that he also had a brush with death on certain occasions. But Jon also knows he has to be brave for his old man sake with protecting his sister's well being. But Jon's thought's was the day that he discovered his mother's and brother in law corpses in the backyard has played numberable times over and over in his head. That alone is his biggest question.

(did that really just happened)? But aleast he's is still alive from Terra tried to kill him at one point and time leaving him for dead. But with much experience in shooting guns and a lot of hunting in the previous years. It's comes to mind when it helps protects the family that's all matter to Jon.

Now Sheila is still in the state of a nervous break down from all that she has been through. Sleeping with her bedroom door opened taking two shower's a day maybe three at the most. Because Ed's filthe has violated her body when Ed had seduce her. Since then that nasty filthe is still there.

Now Sheila is having anxiety attacks from trains sounds and can't go into a store with a lot of people around. And a little jumpy from a passing car. Or a knock at the door she would run to her room. This wasn't the way of the normal for to live their lives and now that Ed is gone for sure with no worries at all. And if Sheila ever get married again it would take a lot for her to trust another man. Sometimes a woman will not trust other mens because of what they being through with the man that's in front of her treating her like crap.

It's harder to find a good woman one because abuses mistreated and set aside. It makes it really tuff for the next man who wants a chance with someone that is so beautiful and what God has made is always good. Even though that word trust must be establish among men as well as a women.

Before moving forward in life's journey. Someone once said that life is like a sorted box of candie that you never would know what you may received. But be careful on how we may look at that between good evil love and hate. That's the candies of life itself to where we may choose and keep in the heart pick and keep so be it. Tomorrow is given to us but not promised hours afterward's.

Therefore life is still great for the Bentford's as putting the pieces that was broken mending together for healing so together and move forward. Now that Ed no longer exist his ways of doing evil will linger from time to time. With his daugther being around so shall his seed be corrupted as he was. But the authoritie has place Terra into a holding camp for girl's that did horrific crimes and for self evaluation. But it doesn't change a thing for Terra to escape to get vengeance on her father's enemies and Sheila for blacking her eyes. While in her cell on a dark and cold night Terra wrote down her plot on getting out. But she needs to align herself with two others that she likes and became friends. Someone that she trust and willing to have her back if nothing else.

Terra knows she has nothing to loose but to think about her revenge on a family that killed her father. As thinking on her plans she noticed in a mirror one night that her eye's turned colors like her darn father's did when stuff isn't right. That's from being upset for what she got caught for killing her boss Dr Letchell and staff. As developing the same attributes as her father but one that is turned invisible.

See Ed quite often injected himself with an serum to make himself invisible when on the locomotive to where the locomotive is driving itself.

Now the Sheriff's office is going to informed the Bentford's on their report with Terra's situation and the locomotive is back with the company it came from. Ed's house would be auction off compensate for the victim's families he killed.

And Ed's corpse's was burned in the coroner crematory. Now that Ed has departed from this life he wouldn't be remember not even his employee's from his auto parts store. By asking them in a individual conversation they thought the man was a good man but was very discreet about his personal life.

Ed's store will go to the court's decision in which Terra is his daugther in which she may inherit the business. But if she's convicted for killing Dr.Letchell and his staff then the court's may auction the building with the business as well.

There's a knock at the front door as Jon answer it and it was a Sheriff deputy to deliver the report "Can I help officer?" ask Jon. "May I come in?" ask the deputy. "i wanted to let you descent folks know that Terra is in a psycho ward for self evaluation before we convict her for her role in the Dr. Letchell office. That locomotive is back where it came from a company called STF (Southern Transit Freight) it's located in South Hunterburg. And Dart's house will be auction off to pay the victims family including you all as well. Mr. Dart's business may be also on the market." all said the Deputy. "I have a questioned." said Jon. "Where's is Ed's remaines?" ask Jon. "Well son you can't see them because he was cremated." said the Deputy. "Yeah!!" said Jon. And Sheila was also very relief from the report on the evil ones.

It was like a load off of her shoulders to know that her father's former foe is gone for good. As Sheila thought that life is better without a person like Ed and his daugther. As the day goes with good news that everyone tends to be in a good mood for a celebration. With the house still in pieces but it's ok. Nothing is going to break the mood the joy that this family has of now.

Now for weeks on edge everything seems normal in the household except for June's absence to where that Jon is sitting in his room on the bed and June walks in and lecture him about his room being reckless. Jon sees his mother in this vision on his bed talking to him. And she disappear as Jon tried to reaches for her while holding back his tears. But he couldn't fill her as he falls on his bed. As Jon wept like never before proven that any man can misses his only mother thats only one and no more after she's gone.

Same as Sam is caught talking to himself in the kitchen having a beer with a sandwich. When Sheila had walked in and wandering who was he talking too. But he admitted by telling Sheila that he misses her mother like crazy It seems to driving Sam crazy at times. But pay him no mind as he would say often. But also it's a struggle trying to put the pieces back togther with a center piece missing. In which June is the articlated pivot point she was the one held everything together. A void that can't and couldn't be filled by another.

Therefore Sheila misses both her husband and mother which Sheila is still mad at Jay for going to the backdoor that night when the creature had invade the house to kill what was in sight and Jay happen to go to the back door to check the roof when the creature decided to take Jay. And Sheila fainted. What a nightmare can do at times when it plays in your mind from times over and over. So Sheila grabs a good book to read to eliminate thoughts of that bad night.

But as the family get ready to brace for very bad news the next day. Sam arose early that morning to go and get takeout breakfast that is because Jon and Sheila slept a little longer then usual. Sam stop for some reason for a newspaper to check to see if anyone has purchase Ed's business. On the front page (young woman escapes group home). And that young woman is missing and no one hasn't seen her. "What the f—k!! Now she is on her way back here!" said Sam. Suddenly Sam goes in to wake both Jon and Sheila to share the bad news with them both. "What!!" said Jon. "i'm going to kill that b—ch!! once and for all!"said Sheila. "I believe she is headed for us." said Sam. "Well I guess i have to take her out like I did her father." Jon said. Only thing different is that she isn't alone. And Terra is very dangerous. She's is using all avenues to her well liking for a ton of revenge.

As minutes later here comes a Deputy to deliver news that the Bentford's are already aware of the situation. With a knock at the front door "Hello folks i just stop to tell you all some bad news."said the Deputy. "You come to tell us this s—t!" Sam said. "Well sir a least you all are aware of it." said the Deputy. "The Sheriff Dept will put a cruiser in the front for a few nights if you would like?" said the Deputy.

But Terra isn't going to make a move just as of yet.She need some destraction to kill Jon first then Sam. But Sheila is going to be her disciple. Terra plans with a dirty thoughts.

With all that this family has being through is get a dose of a bad seed because of Ed's lust for Sheila. Now Terra isn't quite done yet. As She picks up to where her father had left off. The apple doesn't fall far from the tree. Like Father like daughther.

THE END

I hope this book was well indulge in reading a great piece of living in reality. At times we doesn't know how God may bless you in a certain way of life. But having the ability to become a instrument in the publishing field. But having a passion for reading and writing is a God's gift to all mankind.

This is my third book that the Lord God allowed me to bring forth for my audience to enjoy hearing and seeing life as it come at you. The likes of Stephen King James Patterson.

Paul L. Dunbar of Dayton Ohio and there are a few more that has inspired me to write. After years of writing and reading these famous individual works made me realized that I also wanted to become a writer. As a musician would sit and pour his heart mind and soul into a song for fans and all walks of life to listen to. Writer's are the same way but a different world. It's very delightful to work for readers all over the world that may be intriguing with that certain book.

Because the author poured his/ hers minds and souls into getting your approval for a job well done in writing from the heart. May you enjoy this work of literature and may God continue to smile upon you.

Thank you

R L.(Rick) Hutchins